The Boarding School Series #4
The Sheik's Baby Surprise

Elizabeth Lennox

The Boarding School Series Introduction Stories are available as a free e-book from ElizabethLennox.com as well as other e-book retailers.

CONTENTS

Chapter 1

Rule number one: Never buy cheap shoes! Jina cursed herself every step of the steep drive as the shoes she'd bought yesterday, specifically for this event, squished and squeaked in the rain.

Rule number two: Never believe the weather forecast! No rain until this evening, the guy had said. Sunny with a bit of clouds, he'd said! Have a good day, he'd said!

Jina was not having a good day. There was no sunshine with a bit of clouds and she was going to take a hammer to these shoes because simply tossing them into the garbage would never be satisfying enough for the torture her poor toes were enduring right now as she made her way up the steep hill.

Rule number three: Anticipate cobblestone sidewalks!

"Whoever built this sidewalk should be shot and tortured," she mumbled as she pulled her trench coat closer. Her hands were shivering as she held her umbrella over her head, dodging lakes masquerading as puddles and cursing herself for taking this assignment.

Actually, that was a stupid thought because she was too new at her job to jeopardize her reputation by not accepting an assignment. As a translator, and a new one at that, she had to build up her client list before she could get picky about who she worked for.

Oh, that would be a nice fantasy! Some women dreamed about marrying a man and having kids, the white picket fence and a dog running around catching a Frisbee. Jina dreamed about becoming one of the best translators with a client list that would allow her to raise her hourly rate to the point where she could take a taxi to each assignment. With great shoes!

Jina was so wrapped up in her fantasy world that she didn't hear the motors coming up behind her. To be fair, the rain was pouring down so hard that, even if she had been focusing, she probably wouldn't have heard them coming up the curving driveway.

The only reason she realized they were there was because they zoomed past her. And in the process, the first vehicle hit one of those puddle-lakes full on, dousing her body in cold rainwater.

At the first contact, Jina froze, unable to believe, or even understand, what had just happened. Then the second vehicle passed by and she was once again doused. The vehicles were moving so quickly that the icy rainwater hadn't had a chance to re-fill the puddle so only her feet were splashed this time.

Unfortunately, the second splash caused her to turn in horror and fury, facing the threat head on. Big mistake! The third, and largest, vehicle roared passed, a long, black limousine with tinted windows and really heavy tires. The rain had once again drifted into the depression of the driveway and…wham! The rainwater splashed the front of her, some even reaching up to her neck.

Jina closed her eyes and gritted her teeth as she endured the icy trickles of water seeping down her neck, under her black dress and between her breasts…stopping when the droplets soaked onto the material of her bra.

"Fabulous!" she hiss furiously.

By the time the fourth vehicle came through, she had the presence of mind to jump backwards, out of the way of the water. Thinking she'd finally avoided calamity, she breathed a sigh of relief.

Unfortunately, the fates were not finished laughing at her this morning. The cobblestone sidewalk was lined with holly bushes. Perhaps they were planted for security reasons. But as Jina stumbled backwards, her heel unable to find solid ground, she had the sneaking suspicion that the holly bushes had been planted there just to further her own humiliation. Down she fell, an ignominious heap of cold, angry woman battling a prickly bush. And losing the battle!

"You're kidding me!" she yelled, then froze. Anytime she moved, another prickly leaf poked through the material of her coat and dress. There were prickles all over her head and neck and she couldn't even grab onto something to pull herself up because…everything had prickles! She was stuck! She was furious and she wanted to kick some butt. Preferably the butt of the man or woman who had so rudely driven past her, splashed her with pre-winter rain and then created a situation where she'd fallen into this mess.

Carefully, ever so slowly, she wiggled her way closer to the dirt.

Jina was cursing silently when strong hands wrapped around her wrists, lifting her effortlessly out of the prickly, wet mess.

"Whoa!" she gasped, feeling like she was flying for a moment until her feet were once again on the ground, strong, firm hands moving to her waist to steady her and she blinked, trying to understand what had just happened.

"Are you okay?" a deep voice said.

Jina looked around, trying to identify the voice. But in the place where the face of her rescuer should be was only a chest. Looking higher…and higher still, she finally looked into the dark, almost black eyes of the man attached to the hands that were still attached to her waist.

"Whoa!" she said again, but this time her astonishment was caused by the instant impact of this man's eyes on her. It wasn't exactly like an electric shock. It was more along the lines of a hammer slamming into her chest. And pounding repeatedly. Faster and faster.

Oh, that was probably her heartbeat, she finally thought, still staring up at the man.

Malik looked down at the gloriously wet woman with the most astonishingly beautiful eyes. And stared. He probably looked like a fool, but he simply couldn't tear his eyes away from hers. She was beautiful. When she uttered the surprised word, his focus was pulled away from those amazing, crystal blue eyes…her mouth was a work of art, he thought. Small, rosebud lips with a full, pouting lower lip that he instantly wanted to taste, to nibble on. His hands shifted slightly as he realized that he wanted to nibble and taste everywhere on this delectable woman's body. Those eyes! Dark lashes only made the light blue color look almost mystical. And the slant of her eyes made one think of a witch. A seductive, magical witch that could spirit his soul away and he wouldn't give a damn!

When he realized where his fanciful thoughts had taken him, he laughed softly. Scarlett would be proud of him with all of those ridiculous thoughts. But as he stared down at this woman, he didn't feel ridiculous. He wanted her.

He would have her.

"Are you okay?" the deep voice asked.

Was she okay? Jina had no idea. She couldn't feel her toes. She had water dripping down her neck once again because the water droplets from the horrible holly bush had dripped onto her face and neck, her hair probably looked a fright, her face was so wet that her mascara was most likely smeared over her cheeks and…was something sticking out of her head?

Jina pulled back and reached up, grimacing when she pulled a dead branch, filled with additional prickly leaves, out of her hair. "Ow!" she gasped. The green, pointy leaves attached to the branches were bad enough but when these suckers dried out, they were worse than needles!

Tossing the branch behind her, Jina took a deep breath, trying very hard not to burst into tears in front of this devastatingly handsome man.

"I'm fine," she lied, then looked around for her umbrella and…why wasn't she getting wet? She looked up and realized that there was an enormous, black umbrella hovering over both of their heads. When she looked to her left, she discovered a man, a very bulky, very scary looking man, holding an umbrella over both of their heads.

Right and left, she discovered that they were surrounded by those scary men with scarier bulges underneath their scary, dark suits.

"I don't…" she wasn't really sure what to say. She glanced down, looking for her tote bag and umbrella. Both were instantly handed to her. "Thank you," she whispered, feeling a numbness take over where that heat had been when the tall man had been touching her. "I have to go," she stated as firmly as she could. "I appreciate the rescue."

"I will drive you to your destination," the tall man announced.

Jina looked up at him and tried very hard to suppress her anger. She was trembling for some reason, and that hammer was still making her heart pound. She had to get away from this man. It was imperative that her heart stay inside of her chest, which meant that she could not be around this man. He was dangerous. And she didn't think that the word "dangerous" fully defined this man's effect on her.

"No. Thank you."

She tried to step away from him, to be on her way. Crisis over, she was moving on and praying silently that her morning would get better.

"I insist. Our vehicles caused your mishap. I will make it up to you."

Jina had just turned away when he uttered those words. But when she heard them, she was almost stunned by the anger that shot through her body. Perhaps if it hadn't been raining, or if her feet weren't aching on the cobblestone sidewalk. Or maybe if she didn't feel like a wet rag in front of this incredibly handsome man's pristine appearance as he stood under umbrellas held by his servants while she struggled to open her own umbrella once more, broken from the fall, she might have been a touch more cautious in her response. But as it was, she was furious and this man was making her feel like this so he was a legitimate target in her mind.

"You can insist all you like, but I'm not getting into the vehicle that created my current predicament. If your driver had any sort of courtesy, he wouldn't have splashed me. Nor would the second or third have splashed this horrible rainwater all over me and I wouldn't be walking uphill in shoes that could have been used as medieval torture devices, if they could stay put together long enough. And I'm really not happy with the fact that it WASN'T SUPPOSED TO RAIN TODAY!" She was screaming by the end of her rant and didn't care what anyone thought by this point. It was either scream or cry and screaming was marginally more dignified so she took that option with gusto!

Taking a deep breath, she closed her eyes and nodded her chin for emphasis. She felt much better now. Turning around, she ignored the tall, devastatingly attractive man who was still staring at her, praying that no other catastrophe would happen since she suspected that the man was still watching her.

This day was not happening, she told herself as she entered the employee entrance of the embassy where her client was probably already waiting for her. She was ten minutes late, her hair was a dripping mess, her makeup was barely salvageable, her stockings were so badly damaged that there was nothing she could do but take them off and, she stared at her image in the mirror, there was another leaf sticking out of her hair!

She wanted to just hide with mortification. Why couldn't the man have been bald and fat? Why couldn't he have had bad teeth? Or just bad breath?!

No. Today was just not happening. She smoothed her hair back, applying extra pins to make herself look a bit more presentable, dabbed some powder on her nose to hide the redness as she fought to keep herself from bursting into tears, and hurried out into the ballroom where guests were milling about already.

She found her client easily enough and apologized. Thankfully, the woman was gracious and waved away the need for any apology. "I haven't even gone inside, dear. So no harm at all. And you have a very good reputation so I'm thrilled to be working with you today." She gestured towards the event which was already underway. "Shall we?"

Jina forced a smile and tried to relax. This was her job and she was extremely good at it. She had to remind herself that the man, whoever he was, had gone on with his day just as she was about to do with her own.

Stepping out into the ballroom, Jina was pretty sure that fate was laughing hysterically at her.

The man, that man, was standing in the center of the room and her client, the gracious woman who was a legend in the banking industry, was making a beeline for the man in question.

No, Jina thought as her feet were barely able to lift off of the carpeting. This simply wasn't happening. Yes, it was similar to an ostrich sticking its head in the sand but she didn't care. She didn't care about anything, other than not being near this man any longer! No! She wanted to stomp her foot in frustration. She wanted to scream at him to get out. Or even better, she wanted to spin around on her pathetically shoed foot and run away, hide from this man's dangerous, all-knowing look.

But she didn't do any of those things. She was much slower in her approach than her client, but she walked over to the small group of chatting guests, her lashes lowered over her eyes so that she didn't have to look at the man.

Maybe he wouldn't recognize her, she thought to herself. She'd been wet and bedraggled, wearing a dripping trench coat. Oh, and let's not forget those leaves and branches sticking out of her hair! Yes, maybe those had disguised her enough!

She almost laughed at the possibility. Shaking her head mentally, she stood behind her client, praying silently that her translation services would not be needed.

But noooo! That fate thing was still having a blast with her day!

"You seem to have recovered quite well from your trauma," the man commented in Spanish. "And if you look out the windows, you will notice that I have stopped the rain so that your trip home will be significantly easier."

Jina's eyes snapped up to his and she held her breath. Goodness he was devastatingly handsome. But Spanish? He had a darker complexion but...she wouldn't have guessed Spanish from his accent earlier. She would have guessed Middle Eastern.

He said something in Spanish about numbers and she turned to her client, translating the information for her. The woman said something back and Jina turned to the man, staring at his chin.

Jina waited as patiently as possible for the man's response, but there was only silence. Finally, with irritation, she looked up at him, not sure why he wasn't responding.

When the man winked at her, she couldn't stop the blush that formed. "That's better," he said in Spanish. "Your eyes tell me that you're still furious with me, but that's okay. I have it on very good authority that I am gifted at soothing angry tempers."

Jina's mouth dropped open and she glared at the man, shocked by what he was implying. "Are you saying…"

"My stables have many spirited mares. All they need is a firm hand to show them how to behave and they are putty in my hands."

Jina's eyes narrowed. "Are you implying that I am like a horse? An animal?"

Her client's phone buzzed and the woman lifted her hand, excusing herself. Jina's mouth dropped open as she watched her only shield walk away from her.

Standing in the middle of a crowd, she felt her heartbeat increase, her mind frantically trying to find a way to get away from this man. When her client disappeared into the hallway, she glanced back up at the tall man, her stomach cringing with the triumphant look in his eyes.

"It appears that it is just you and me now," he told her, switching to English.

Jina shook her head. "No. I am definitely not standing here with you."

"I know you're afraid," he commented, taking her hand and tucking it onto his arm, leading her through the people. "But there is no need to be nervous."

"I'm not afraid of you!" she lied. She wasn't really afraid, so much as terrified out of her mind. Why could he make her feel so much with just a touch? What was it about this man in particular that got her so riled up in different ways? It was a mystery that she didn't even want to solve. He was the enemy! He was one of those wealthy people who thought he could move through life with impunity and she avoided them like the plague.

"I'm not afraid of you, sir," she said with as much calm as she could muster under the circumstances. "I just don't want to speak with you.'

"That's too bad," he tsked. "Because we're going to talk. And we're going to get to know each other."

Jina pulled back but he simply placed a hand over hers, keeping her hand trapped by his. "No. We're not. You don't seem to understand, sir. I don't like you. I don't like what you represent and I definitely don't like the way you are manipulating this situation. Every step you take, forcing me to follow you, is only reinforcing my dislike of you."

Malik chuckled, surprised by the vehemence in her voice. And he had no doubt that she was being completely honest with him. Oh, she was affected by him. Just as powerfully as he was affected by her. And they would eventually become lovers. But he was definitely going to enjoy the challenge of understanding this woman. A novel experience, he thought. He rarely cared to understand his lovers except for what they wanted in bed.

But this woman, he wanted to understand completely. "So tell me, what has made you such a cynic of men in this world?"

She clenched her teeth tightly. "Perhaps it is the way they manipulate the rest of the world to suit their purposes?" she suggested, looking around at the way they were now in an isolated area of the ballroom. "Or maybe it is your arrogance in thinking that I want to be alone with you."

He shook his head. "I am very aware that you do not want to be alone with me, my dear. But perhaps we should first introduce ourselves before we continue our mating dance."

She gasped and pulled back. "I am not dancing with you! And mating…" she struggled to even say the word, it was so out of the realm of possibilities. "That's definitely not going to happen."

He leaned closer, slipping his hands into his pockets. "Ah, you're just throwing out more challenges. I think I should warn you, I truly love a good challenge."

She cringed inwardly. He did look the kind of man who would rise to any challenge placed in front of him. "You're like a bull with a red flag, aren't you?'

He chuckled softly. "Oh, you have no idea. And your red flag is snapping and catching my attention."

Jina's body was trembling, her muscles tense with a strange feeling. This man was too confident for her. And too arrogant. So why was she so painfully aware of him as a man? Why couldn't she simply give him a polite set-down and move on with her job? "Please, just leave me alone," she told him firmly and started to walk back into the ballroom.

"I can't do that," he said, stopping her retreat with his words.

"You can. You just won't."

He shrugged one of those massive shoulders encased in a perfectly tailored suit. "However you'd like to define it. We're not finished."

She looked away, unable to hold his confident gaze. "Even if I ask you politely?"

He smiled slightly. "You could try it."

Jina knew that he wouldn't care how prettily she wrapped up her request, he was going to try and pursue her. "Well, then, I guess the race is on, sir."

She walked away at that point, feeling strong and powerful since she'd gotten in the last word.

Jina spied her client just as the woman walked back into the ballroom and headed in her direction.

The woman smiled at Jina. "What do you think of our guest of honor?" she asked in a sly voice.

Jina looked back at her, not sure what she meant. "Who is the guest of honor?" she asked, but she knew! It was him!

The woman nodded at the man who was staring right back at Jina, a look in his eyes that told her that she hadn't had the last word. Not by a long shot!

"That is Sheik Malik Amari del Nader of Sarkit, one of the most powerful men in the region." The woman chuckled as they both watched Malik as he lifted his glass to them from across the room. "And a charmer if ever there was one."

Jina's mouth fell open slightly. She'd known that he was powerful but, good grief! A sheik? Couldn't he have been simply a prince or something boring and obnoxious? Why did he have to be the head honcho of everyone? Even neighboring countries followed his lead!

"Oh no!" Jina murmured.

"What's wrong?"

Jina pulled her gaze away from the man and turned so that her back was to him. It didn't stop her awareness of the man, she could still feel the heat of his gaze, but at least she wasn't facing him any longer. That was something, she told herself.

"I yelled at him," Jina finally admitted.

The other woman laughed and clapped her hands together. "Oh, this is going to be a delicious afternoon!" she said. "Let's go," and she surged into the crowd once more.

Jina thought that she was going to be dragged right back to the man's group, but her client had business to conduct and moved towards her prey, mingling with the other guests. By the end of the event, the woman had accomplished some amazing victories and Jina was in awe of the woman's negotiating skills.

"You were wonderful," her client said, shaking Jina's hands. "I can't wait to work with you again." A twinkle entered the older woman's eyes. "But I think you have some unfinished business, don't you?"

Jina refused to look over at the man who had been staring at her. Every time she looked up, the man was in her line of sight. All afternoon, he'd tormented her, tried to distract her. But she'd won! She'd finished her job and she'd done well despite his annoying habit of always glancing her way. And her irritating habit of reacting with a shiver every time she looked back at him.

"Not at all. If you don't need me any longer today..." The woman glanced behind Jina's shoulder. "Oh, I don't think so." A moment later, the woman was gone and Jina was left trembling with awareness.

Malik watched the fascinating woman her facial expressions and body movements, the way her eyes flashed from one person to another. It was all so fascinating! He also loved the way this woman tried to hide her femininity. Those rosebud lips, covered in a neutral lipstick, couldn't hide the sensuousness of her nature.

He was doubly impressed when he listened to her translations. Never before had he heard a translator come across with such precision, such attention to detail. First, he would have her in his bed. When he was tired of her, which would inevitably happen, he would hire her on as a staff member. She was exceptionally beautiful and amazingly talented. A perfect combination for his bed and his staff.

He would start by taking every single one of those pins out of her long dark hair, tangling his fingers through the soft tresses. He would then take her to one of the exclusive boutiques in Paris, drape her lush figure in soft fabrics. He also wouldn't mind taking a knife to that's drab, shapeless black dress that she was currently wearing. The ridiculous garment covered her from her neck all the way down to below her knees. A woman with a figure like that should be wearing silks and lace. She should be hovering over him as she debated which part of his body to caress with that rosebud mouth of hers.

Malik took a deep breath and pulled his gaze away from his current prey. His body was reacting too strongly to this woman. He never lost control! But with this beauty, with her soft, lilting voice translating the melodic Spanish to her client, his body couldn't help but become interested.

So instead of watching her, he let his eyes drift over the rest of the guests at the function. There were several other world leaders here tonight. None of whom he really wished to speak with at the moment. He supposed that he should mingle a bit more, but after having seen that woman, hearing her voice, he dismissed all of the political issues he needed to deal with at the moment. His entire focus was on planning this woman's seduction.

Free at last! Jina set her cup of coffee down on a nearby table and moved towards the door. The opposite door from where that horrible man was standing. She wanted nothing to do with him. As she slipped behind another group of lingering guests, she forced her eyes to look only towards the doorway. Escape. There was absolutely no way that she was going to allow herself to scan the room one more time. Every time she done that over the past two hours, her eyes had clashed with that man's dark gaze. She was finished with him! She was finished with all of the arrogant men who thought that they had the right to simply buy a woman for the night. Oh, she supposed that money rarely exchanged hands. It probably happened occasionally, but the women in this room were after a bigger prize. And the men in this room knew what the ultimate prize was.

She wasn't ready for marriage though. And even if she was, the men in this room thought themselves too high and mighty for a simple working girl like her. She knew her place in the caste system. The men and women that attended functions like this with the movers and shakers of the world - they were the powerbrokers, the wealthy and influential women and men who made the decisions that affected people like her. She would not be offered a position as a wife. No, her offers would be much lower on the social hierarchy. Too often in her line of work, the men assumed she was available for additional "services". That offended her!

She wouldn't mind so much if the men would just accept her professional capacity. But too often, the men thought that she was theirs for the taking, they just needed to come up with the right price. It was more than a little disgusting, but it was also just one of the trials of her job. She'd have to learn to deal with that aspect diplomatically.

Jina hurried down the hallway to the locker room where the employees and consultants could store their coats and purses in lockers. She quickly unlocked the door and slipped inside, eager to get home and slip into something more comfortable. She was still a bit damp from her miserable arrival earlier today and dreamed of a pair of slippers, sweat pants and a bulky sweatshirt. All dry!

She had less than two hours until her next assignment so she hurriedly opened her locker, grabbed her purse and her rain jacket as well as the pathetic excuse for an umbrella. The rain had died down during the event, but she could once again hear the thunder booming. She only wished that she'd remembered to bring a different pair of shoes. She never should have bought such cheap, suede shoes. Or more specifically, wanna-be suede. They'd looked so good in the store though!

With a sigh, she stepped out through the employees' door and popped the button on her umbrella that lifted the protection over her head, cringing as the metal blades expanded with reluctance.

"Great," she mumbled under her breath. A broken umbrella, barely wearable shoes and a damp dress. "Lovely day." Dark, mysterious eyes popped into her mind but she pushed them away. She wasn't going to think about that man any more. He'd taken up way too much headspace already.

Looking down at her shoes, she wished she'd spent her money more wisely. Jina wasn't sure if these pathetic pumps would make it all the way to her house. It wasn't as if she'd paid $1000 for a pair of Prada shoes. Not that she wouldn't love to be able to afford a pair of beautiful Prada pumps but that wasn't in her budget at this stage of her career. A cheap pair of black suede shoes that fit her feet was about all she could handle at the moment. Soon! Her client base was growing, people were requesting her now. Very soon, she would be able to increase her hourly rates and make more money.

Still under the small protection of the overhead canopy, she looked out at the torrential rains with resignation. This was going to be a mess. The subway was still five blocks away. She'd have to make a dash for it or she'd be drenched no matter what. The shoes were the least of her worries now that she realized how hard it really was raining.

"May I offer you a ride?" a deep voice said from her left.

No! She'd left him behind at the party! She absolutely refused to believe that he was standing behind her right now! The shiver of awareness that raced down her spine as the chocolatey, deep voice reverberated through her body caused her anger to increase tenfold.

Turning to her left she glared at the man. Well, she tried to glare at him! Her glare missed the mark by about a foot. In reality, she was only glaring at his chest. Again.

Tilting her head up a bit higher, she increased the intensity of the fury coming through her gaze. But she had to remind herself that she was a professional, this could be a potential client. Not that she would actually accept any work from this man. No way! He was too arrogant and conceited for her to be able to stand working with someone like him. But she didn't want to burn bridges. She had a reputation that she needed to maintain in the political world and making an enemy of a man as powerful as this one would be a bad career move.

Smoothing out the anger and banking her rising temper, she took a deep breath and forced her lips to smile. "Thank you so much for the offer, sir. But I'm perfectly fine. I do need to rush, though."

She started to leave but a hand reached out to stop her. Normally, she would simply offer another smile and move around the hindrance. But at this man's first touch, the heat from his hand burned through the thick layer of her raincoat as well as the sleeve of her dress. She imagined that the skin underneath his long, strong fingers would have red burn marks where his fingers were now lying.

She opened her mouth to say something to him, wanting to give him a very polite sat down. She should firmly tell him that she was not for sale and needed to be on her way. But something in his dark eyes stopped her. Her mouth opened, her blue eyes widened ever so slightly, and she was struck dumb by the intense heat that permeated through her body as he stepped closer to her.

She wasn't used to that kind of height in the men that she dated nor in the men that she worked with in a professional capacity. Normally the men that she worked with were either shorter than she was or just about the same height. She even had to wear flat shoes occasionally so that she didn't tower over some of the men. But this man was extremely tall! Even in her heels, the top of her head didn't even reach his chin. That realization was a bit disconcerting. It gave him additional power over her, a power that she didn't like to relinquish.

Jina shivered as the man continued to look down at her. "Thank you for the offer, but I'll be fine."

"It is raining hard and it is a long walk to the parking lot. You had a traumatic walk here earlier today. Please, let me drive you to your car."

Jina shook her head and took a step back, feeling crowded by his height and his heat. "I sincerely appreciate your offer," she lied, "but I can get home on my own steam."

She started to walk around him once again but he shook his head. "It is raining harder than earlier. Let me help you. I owe you that much at least because of my chauffer's splash on you before you arrived."

Jina couldn't help the laughter that bubbled up inside of her. For some reason, this just struck her as funny. "You're not really going to step in front of me every time I try to go around you, are you?" she asked, looking up into his dark eyes, trying to ignore that crazy, fluttering sensation in her tummy.

And then he smiled. His white teeth were startling against his tanned skin. And even those dark, devilish eyes lit up with humor. "I think I am." He crossed his arms over his massive chest. "What are you going to do about it?"

Jina giggled. Good grief, she never giggled. Smothering her humor, she stepped back. "I think we're going to stand out here in the rain for a quite a while. Because there is no way you're going to get me into that limousine. If you're just as stubborn as I am, then we're playing a game that might never end."

He chuckled as well. "I can be much more stubborn." His eyes narrowed. "And I think I'm probably more diabolical."

She laughed again. What was it about this man? She hated his attitude, didn't she? "I'm sure that you probably got away with a lot of things in your youth that you think can happen again. But I promise you, I won't stand for it. And even worse, I'll make a scene." She grinned. "I wanted to major in theatre in college. So I'm pretty good."

Malik laughed again, enchanted by this woman and her not-so-dire threats. "So we are at an impasse. How can we resolve this situation?"

Jina lifted her purse higher onto her shoulder and crossed her arms over her chest, imitating his stance. "Well, here's the deal. I believe you're trying to ask me out on a date, correct?"

He was actually trying to get her into his bed, but he could go along with a "date". To start. "Yes."

"The problem here is that I don't date wealthy men."

His eyes widened in surprise. "You have a problem with money?"

She shook her head. "Not money. No. I have a problem with the personalities that excess wealth creates in people." Her eyes sharpened as she said, "It creates an arrogance that is unattractive."

Malik leaned forward slightly. "You are attracted to me."

Jina opened her mouth to deny that claim, but the words wouldn't come out. "Regardless, your arrogance overwhelms whatever other aspects of you I might, or might not," she added in quickly when she saw the triumphant look in his eyes, "feel towards you. And there's the problem of your arrogance letting you think you can do things with impunity. That really bothers me."

All humor left his features with her claim. "Who has created this fear in you?" he demanded.

Jina was stunned by the instantaneous change in his demeanor. "No one has done anything to me personally." One shoulder went up and down. "We hear stories in this profession. While mingling with the powerful and elite, there are stories when women are hurt or attacked. Because of the man's position, she is not believed when she reports the abuse." She looked down. "I'm not putting myself into that kind of a position," she said firmly.

His arms dropped and he eliminated the space between them. "When we make love, my beauty, I promise that you will not be hurt. It will only be pleasure."

Jina swallowed. She heard the finality in his tone and his words but rejected his assertion that it was only a matter of "when", not "if" she made love with this man. "That's not going to happen."

He lifted his hand, running a finger down her cheek. "I believe that it is inevitable," he contradicted. "Something this intense cannot be ignored."

Under other circumstances, Jina would roll her eyes and slap his hand away from her skin. But right now, this moment, the fire on her skin from his touch was sending crazy thoughts ricocheting around her body and she almost swayed closer, wanting more contact with this man than just his fingers.

When she realized what she'd almost done, she shook her head and stepped back again. "No. Nothing is inevitable. We control our actions with…" she had trouble remembering how her actions were controlled. "We control our actions through conscious thought and intentional communications with another person. There is no force that is inevitable besides gravity."

The deep chuckle that emanated from this man sent unexpected and unwanted desire spiraling through her once again.

"You are young and, I'm guessing, haven't had many lovers. But we will be together, my beauty."

Jina lifted her hand to pull his away, but her fingers stopped when they wrapped round his wrist. They stood like that for a long moment, just staring at each other. Jina could barely breathe as the heat from his eyes warmed her.

When he finally pulled away, Jina actually opened her mouth, prepared to demand that he put his hand right back against her cheek. She felt…bereft…without his touch. She wanted the heat back!

She shook her head when she realized what she was thinking and snapped her mouth closed. Good grief! Was she losing her mind?

"I have to go," she whispered, wishing her voice was stronger, more assertive. But all she could manage was a whisper even after she cleared her throat.

He didn't stop her this time and she ran across the pavement towards the street, ignoring the cold splatters of rain as they hit her legs. Her shoes would be ruined, but that was a small price to pay for peace of mind.

When she descended the stairs to the subway, she took a deep breath as she folded her umbrella and sat down on the metal bench to wait for the subway to arrive. The whole time she sat there, her eyes didn't see her surroundings. Nor did she realize that the trains were coming to the station, then departing after letting off people and taking on new passengers. She was simply too stunned by her encounter with the man to let anything into her head other than replaying their conversation over and over again.

It took about three trains coming and going from the station before she realized what she was doing. Just sitting here? Was she crazy? She was in

New York City! People were hurt or killed when they didn't pay attention to their surroundings!

She stood up, ignoring the squishy feeling every time she took a step in her cheap shoes. When the train arrived, she stepped into the closest car and took a seat, grateful that it was the early afternoon and she didn't have to stand as the commuters filled up all the available spaces in their rush to get home.

When she emerged from the subway in her neighborhood, she trudged along the street to her building, her mind still going over their conversation again and again. She had to push him out of her mind. There wouldn't be another encounter with the tall, dark devil so she should just stop thinking about him, push those dangerous eyes out of her mind. He was gone. He was in the past. Her dark stranger was history!

Finally reaching her building, she pulled the old, wooden door open and trudged up the stairway to her apartment. Her mind was thinking about warm sweatpants and a hot cup of tea. Yes, tea would solve all of her problems and warm her up from the inside out. Tea fixed everything, she told herself.

Jina stood in front of her doorway, staring at the elaborately decorated bag. It was from him. She had no idea how she knew it, but she was positive that, whatever was in that bag, was from THAT MAN.

With keys dangling from her cold fingers, she continued to stare at the package, wondering what she should do. She couldn't accept a gift from him. She wasn't a government worker and the man wasn't a client, so it wasn't a question of professional ethics. It was just…a gift! From him!

A door slammed on one of the other floors, snapping her out of her focus on the bag. It was just a bag. She could return it to him with a firm explanation that she did not accept gifts under any circumstances.

Yes, that was what she would do!

Taking her keys in her hand, she unlocked her apartment door and grabbed the package. Setting it on the countertop, she ignored it for all of fifteen minutes. Just long enough to toss her cheap shoes into the garbage and hang her wet coat up on a hook to dry. She'd need her coat for tonight's assignment and didn't relish the idea of wearing a wet coat over her black cocktail dress. Of course, the cocktail dress she normally wore was almost exactly like her black sheath dress, just with a better fabric. Both dresses were demure, allowing her to blend into the background. She didn't want to stand out when she was working. It was bad for business because the ladies at these high-powered functions didn't want to be out-done by the hired help.

She made herself a cup of tea, staring at the colorful package while she waited for the water to warm up. When she was leaning a hip against the countertop, a steaming cup of blackberry tea in her hands, she sighed, resigned to opening the package. She'd never been able to resist a secret. It simply wasn't in her power to not look inside that bag.

When she pulled out the tissue paper, her heart was beating frantically. The box inside the beautiful bag looked suspiciously like...oh no! He hadn't!

Jina's fingers shook as she pulled the box out of the bag. A shoebox! A Christian Louboutin shoebox!

"Please please..." she chanted to herself as she slowly, reverently, opened the box. At the last moment, she closed her eyes, actually afraid to see what decadent luxury was inside that box.

When she opened her eyes and looked down, the breath whooshed out of her. Sitting in the box, looking innocuous and perfect, were black suede pumps with the trademark red sole.

Jina's fingers shook as she lifted one perfect shoe out of the box. They were stunningly beautiful. They were also about two inches higher than the heels she normally wore but that didn't matter. They were still perfect.

She lifted the other shoe out of the box, staring at the pair. She shouldn't touch them, she thought, even as she carried them over to her small den. Slipping the shoes onto her feet, she was stunned to realize that they actually fit! How had the man guessed her shoes size? Impossible! The man was the devil, she thought. That was the only answer. He was Satan sent here to tempt her with a beautiful, and surprisingly comfortable, pair of perfect, black heels!

Jina looked over at the bedraggled pair of shoes sticking out of her garbage can that were no longer wearable. Not after the soaking they took today.

She walked to her bedroom, careful to stay on the carpet so she didn't mess up the soles. When she saw the way the heels made her legs look, she couldn't believe it! They were stunning! And her legs looked...long!

Jina shook her head. She couldn't keep these shoes. Regretfully, she pulled the shoes off and stored them carefully back in the tissue paper, then the box. She peered into the box, looking for a card but there was nothing. She wasn't even sure where the shoes were bought.

And a more disturbing thought, how had the man known her address? What kinds of resources could the man call upon to get her address so quickly?

That should feel wrong. Strange. But in a weird, crazy way, it actually warmed her.

Jina stood up in horror when that thought hit her mind. Good grief, what was she thinking? The man stalked her, probably spoke to her agency who gave him the information on her address, and sent her some shoes. He was doing exactly what she'd just told him she hated! The man had the power to get her agency to reveal personal information! Or he'd done it some other way. Normal people simply didn't have the resources to find other people's addresses. Not unless they were weirdo hackers or stalkers!

So she absolutely was not feeling warmed by the idea that the man had broken laws in order to get her address. She was irritated and disturbed! Yes, the fluttering in her stomach was all about how she didn't like the man and the obnoxious power he had.

Stuffing the bag into her large tote, she would figure out how to return the shoes somehow. She'd just take them to the Louboutin store over on Fifth Avenue. She wasn't exactly sure where the store might be on Fifth Avenue, but all of the upscale vendors had a storefront on that street. If he hadn't bought them there, she'd just hand them over to...well, a homeless person always needed a new pair of shoes, she thought with relish. Yes, she'd love to see that man's reaction when he saw a homeless person wearing the outlandishly expensive pair of shoes.

How dare he! She stomped over to her shower and stepped into the tepid water, letting out a yelp of pain as the cooler than expected water hit her already cold skin. But she was too angry to step out of the shower. She blamed that on the stranger as well, irritated beyond belief at a man who could invade her privacy in such a way.

She squeezed shampoo into her hands and lathered her hair, thinking about the shoes. And the man. And how handsome he was. Well, and how beautiful the shoes were.

When she realized her thoughts were straying again, she grabbed her conditioner and lathered her hair, using more energy than she normally would. She finished her shower in record time, despite the fact that she hadn't even intended to shower. She'd taken a shower this morning and now she'd just have to dry her hair and redo her makeup.

The man was making her crazy!

When she pulled her black cocktail dress on, zipping up the back and smoothing her hair once more, she glanced at her shoe choices in her closet. The only other pair she had that would work would be the red shoes. But she couldn't wear red shoes tonight! How outrageous! Her eyes glanced through her bedroom doorway where the beautiful shoes were laying innocently in the box.

No! She pulled her gaze away and slipped on a pair of strappy, black sandals. They weren't comfortable, but they would work for the night. She stashed a pair of sneakers into her black tote bag, knowing from past experience, not to mention her current day's shoe debacle, that she'd need them by the end of the night.

Actually, she slipped her strappy shoes off of her feet and pulled on her sneakers. No reason to traipse through the city in the rain one more time and ruin another pair of shoes. Her sneakers would be wet when she came home that night, but at least they would be a lot more comfortable than the heels would be.

She walked by the Louboutin bag, refusing to even look at it this time. She yanked her apartment door open and walked out, her still-damp raincoat over her arm and her tote bag filled with anything she might need for the evening's assignment. She was translating French tonight for a diplomat at a cocktail party, a relatively easy assignment.

Hurrying out of the apartment, she clenched her teeth as she dove right back out into the rain. Her umbrella was only able to keep the rain off of her head. The downpour was still too heavy to do much more and her umbrella had pretty much given up on trying to be strong. It had taken too much abuse already today and was protesting more effort. Thankfully, her raincoat protected her dress and, since she was smart enough to wear sneakers instead of shoes this time around, her feet would be wet, but her shoes wouldn't be ruined.

When she arrived at the event site, she ducked through the employee entrance and showed her credentials. Getting through security seemed a bit more problematic than usual but she endured the trouble, knowing that the guards were only doing their jobs. There were a lot of important, political leaders at many of the events at which she worked and there was no use getting annoyed at their security measures. She accepted it as just part of the job.

When she was finally through the security area and able to find a locker in which to store her purse, she smoothed her hair back into place and took a deep breath. Attaching her badge to her dress, she worked her way through the catering staff and smiled at the other translators, several of whom she'd worked with in the past. When she reached the area in which the "party" was to take place, she scanned the room, glancing down at her cell phone to verify the name of her client. When she found her, Jina introduced herself and asked if there were any specific issues the woman wanted Jina to watch out for.

Jina understood that her client, a finance director for one of the major banks, was here to negotiate business terms for a French conglomerate and they talked briefly about the other guests. Jina was more than willing to step back when another guest arrived, eager to greet her client.

It was during one of these conversations that Jina just knew that the man, the very man she'd been trying to push out of her mind all afternoon and evening, had arrived. Why he was at this particular gathering, she didn't know, nor did she care. All she knew was that her heart rate picked up into a crazy rhythm and she looked around, trying to hide herself so that he couldn't know that she was here. For some reason, knowing that he was close by terrified her. All the muscles in her body tightened in anticipation and she wanted to duck behind the marble column of the banquet room so that he couldn't see her.

All of her efforts to appear non-descript were for naught though. She was peering around the marble column and her eyes searched for him in the room. And he was staring right at her.

Was he laughing at her efforts to hide from him?

Of course he was!

Her anger over his amusement was deep. But she was cowering. She was being absolutely ridiculous because this man had no power over her. He was just a man. He was no different from the person standing next to her discussing some sort of gardening technique!

Okay, that was completely wrong. The man next to her was about a hundred pounds overweight, most of it centered on his belly. He also sported a beard which, Jina guessed, was used to hide the man's jowls and extra chins

21

caused by his additional weight. And he was drunk. Horribly, horrendously drunk.

As Jina stared across the room, she looked at the dangerous stranger and knew that there wasn't a superfluous ounce of weight on the man's tall, muscular body. And there was no need for the dark haired stranger to sport a beard either. In fact, hiding that granite-hard jaw would be a crime.

Tearing her eyes away, she once again focused on the person to which her client was speaking, trying to listen carefully. At the right moment, she stepped forward to translate and give a response. Back and forth she translated for the banker.

Jina watched with growing horror as her stranger moved closer, his eyes daring her to run from him. She thought about it. She really did! But in the end, she couldn't abandon her client. And he knew it, darn him!

Charm oozed out of the man as he lifted his client's hand to his lips. "Good evening, Marianne. How is the banking business lately?" he asked, pretending to focus only on the woman who was sixty if she was a day, and blushing at the attention this stranger was giving to her.

Jina felt better knowing that she wasn't the only woman that this man affected. Even the older woman couldn't resist his personality. She patted herself on the back as she moved into the background once again. Yes, she noticed the way his body shifted ever so slightly, indicating that he would deal with her next, but she didn't care. This was her job, her professional capacity was to blend into the background when a client was speaking. He couldn't fault her for that. Nor would she allow him to interfere with her work. The man could just…go away, she thought with relish.

"Ah Your Highness, ever the charmer, aren't you?" Marianne laughed, still holding onto the man's hand.

"I would never even attempt to charm someone as sophisticated as you are, Marianne. You are lovelier than ever. What brings you to this tedious affair?"

Right away, Marianne's eyes sharpened and Jina's mind shifted gears. Having been in this business for a while now, Jina immediately understood what had just happened. Marianne had only been speaking to the French until she could reach this man. Now her real business of the night began. As they quickly discussed numbers, Jina stepped further into the shadows. The amounts they were discussing were far out of her mind's ability to understand, the financial terms and acronyms beyond her financial knowledge.

After thirty minutes of flirting and haggling, the man once again bowed low over Marianne's hand. "Contact my office in the morning and we'll get started."

Jina blinked. That was it? He was giving in to Marianne's ideas? What had just happened here? She had no idea how that had just worked but she suspected that important business had just transpired.

Marianne smiled up at the man, then glanced over her shoulder at Jina. "Now that we're finished, I'm going to walk away and let you get on with your real reason for coming over to talk to me."

Jina opened her mouth to protest, but the woman only laughed softly and walked away.

Glancing up at the man, then at her client, she clamped her mouth shut, irritated that he was interfering in her job. "I'm following my client," she told him through gritted teeth.

The man had the audacity to reach out to stop her. "Your client is leaving for the night. She finished her business and she is tired." He took her hand and pulled it onto his arm, leading her over to the buffet table. "Now that we are finally alone, tell me about yourself."

Jina watched the doorway. Sure enough, her client was pulling on her coat and walking out the door. Marianne lifted her hand, indicating that Jina was finished and then walked out of the room.

Jina looked up at the man, furious with him for cornering her in this manner. "Since my client is done for the night, I am free to leave."

The man chuckled but wouldn't release her hand. "You don't want to leave."

She glared up at him, ignoring the shiver of awareness. Eventually, they would stop happening, wouldn't they? "Oh, yes I do!"

He shook his head and handed her a plate. "If you leave, then you won't be able to berate me for sending you the gift. Wouldn't you prefer to have your target in front of you when you admonish me for doing something that you didn't like?"

She watched in fascination as he filled the plate with all of the delicious looking appetizers that she'd seen floating around the event all night. She was starving, having been too angry earlier to eat lunch and hadn't thought to grab a snack before coming here.

"I can't eat this," she told him, trying to pull the plate away before he could put a square of cheesecake with what looked like some sort of caramel sauce on it.

He only pulled her plate back towards the table and placed the bite on the corner, then added several other delicacies. "Of course you can. You need your strength. Otherwise your fury won't have power behind it."

Jina wanted to laugh. The man was actually telling her to fill up on food so that she could properly yell at him? Who was this man?

"Who are you?" she asked, more curious than angry now.

"I'm the man who has better taste in shoes than you do," he told her and plunked another sweet on the plate.

"Stop doing that!" she snapped at him, astounded by the amount of food on the plate.

Of course, he ignored her and placed another piece of chocolate on the only empty space. "I'm a growing boy. I need my energy."

She rolled her eyes. "I thought this was for me so that I'd have the energy to yell at you."

"It is," he said and put more on the plate. "But I'll need sustenance to endure the trials of your anger."

When he started to put more on the plate, she shook her head and pulled the plate away. "There's enough on this plate for three people. No more."

He chuckled but conceded. "Fine. We'll come back for second helpings." With that, he took her hand, tugging her towards the end of the buffet table where the utensils were wrapped up in starched linen napkins. He grabbed two and pulled her over to one of the tables in one corner, out of the way from others.

"This will work," he told her and set everything down, then pulled out a chair for her. "My lady," he teased.

"I'm not eating with you." She stood there staring at him.

Malik loved the challenge she shot at him. "Ah, you want to kiss me. I understand." With that, he pushed the chair in and started towards her.

Jina's heart went into overdrive. "No kissing!" she hissed, leaning back and glancing around at the others. Thankfully, they were far enough away from the others sitting at the small table that no one noticed.

His only response was a derisive lifting of his black eyebrow, waiting for her to take the chair.

Jina harrumphed, but pulled out the chair and sat down. She didn't take the offered fork though, refusing to eat even though she was actually starving.

"Suit yourself," he replied and stabbed a crab puff. "This is delicious," he told her. "So tell me all about Jina Thomas. What are your likes and dislikes?" He lifted the fork to stop her words. "And I can't be one of your dislikes," he teased, knowing exactly where her mind was going.

Jina's mouth snapped shut and she glared at him for a long moment while he chuckled softly again. "I don't like arrogant men who manipulate situations to their benefit."

He lifted his finger at that. "Now, that's not fair. There isn't anyone alive who doesn't manipulate situations to suit their needs."

She rolled her eyes. "Are you saying there are no altruistic motivations in the world?"

He shrugged and stabbed a delicious looking piece of chicken in a savory sauce. "I'm saying that it is rare."

Jina couldn't endure watching him eat any longer. She was too hungry and this man just sparked her temper and her appetite. In so many ways!

Grabbing a fork, she stabbed one of the appetizers and popped it into her mouth, not answering immediately. She figured she needed to think carefully about her response before she uttered another word. But as she chewed the delicious food, he continued to watch her. Or more specifically, he watched her lips. And she grew self-conscious as she ate, not to mention hot. Yes, she was decidedly warmer under his intent gaze.

Swallowing took great effort. "Didn't your mother ever tell you that it is rude to stare?" she asked, wishing that her voice was more sarcastic. It sounded all breathy and sexy, even to her ears.

Most likely to his as well since those dark eyes snapped to her blue ones.

"My mother would think you are extremely charming. And my father would appreciate what a beautiful woman you are and would excuse my behavior."

She wasn't sure what to say to that. Her eyes lowered and she remembered the shoes. "I can't accept your gift."

Malik wanted to laugh at how revealing her eyes were. Everything she was feeling or thinking was reflected in those pretty, blue depths. Cornflower, he thought. Her eyes were the same color as the cornflower that he used to see in the fields of Virginia when he was at school.

"What gift would that be?" he asked softly. He stabbed another shrimp and offered it to her. He didn't expect her to accept it so he was pleasantly surprised when she took the fork. Although she only twirled it in her fingers.

"The shoes. The beautiful shoes," she took a deep breath and let it out slowly. "I can't accept the shoes."

The corners of his lips lifted slightly. Not a full smile but, when her eyes glanced up into his dark gaze, she knew that he was laughing at her once again.

"Did someone send you a pair of shoes?" he asked. "Seems slightly outrageous."

She agreed with him. "Yes. Well, they are lovely. And I thank you for the shoes. But they are too expensive. I can't accept them."

"I don't know what you're talking about. You must have an admirer that realized that your shoes were ruined in the storm this afternoon. Perhaps you should have accepted my ride home today and your other shoes wouldn't have been ruined."

Jina laughed but shook her head. "You're being deliberately obtuse, but I know you're the one who sent them."

"I don't know what you're talking about."

Her mouth twisted. "Yes. Well, I'll have to return them. Your account will be credited."

"What account? I have no idea what you're telling me. I didn't send you any shoes, my beauty."

She looked up at him. "Look, I don't really know you and I don't accept gifts from strangers," she told him firmly.

He lifted her hand with his long fingers, tangling with hers and making the breath catch in her throat. "I'm just a man who is interested in a very beautiful and extremely stubborn, cynical woman."

"You're royal," she pointed out.

"I'm just a man, Jina."

She wouldn't let him get away with that. "If you're just a man, how did you find out where I live? And how do you know my name? I didn't tell you my name this afternoon."

A smile! At last a real smile. "Okay, so I'm a man with resources."

"Marianne called you 'Your Highness'. You're the Sheik of Sarkit."

She watched him carefully and suspected that he wasn't going to respond. But when he lifted his eyes from their hands, she held her breath again.

"Yes, I'm from Sarkit."

Jina heard the words. Her eyes narrowed on his features as news clippings suddenly tumbled through her mind. Little by little, the pictures to those news articles connected. When the reality of his identity hit her, she gasped and pulled her hands away from his.

"You really are Sheik Amari del Nader!" and she actually pushed her chair further back.

Malik sighed, frustrated that she now knew his identity. He had been enjoying the anonymity for once. And he definitely didn't like the fear in her eyes. "What difference does my position make between us? We are still attracted to each other and you will still be in my bed once I can overcome your concerns."

She shook her head and stood up. "There's no way you can overcome my concerns," she mocked, angry now. "You're one of the big fish in the big ocean. Sarkit is one of the most powerful countries in the region and you're the most powerful ruler of all of them." She pulled her fingers away when he stood up as well and reached for her. "Are you just playing with me?"

"Why would you think that?" he asked, irritated with her assumptions.

"Just having a bit of fun with the poor, country girl, right?"

His eyes narrowed at her accusation. "I never once implied that you were of lesser intelligence if that's what you're talking about."

She still shook her head, too stunned at the idea that she was standing here speaking with a man of his power and position. "You're…you're…" She looked around, terrified now that she knew who he was. He was Sheik of Sarkit! He had meetings with the president! Good grief, he had meetings with everyone!

"Jina stop right now!" he ordered. When she froze, he muttered a curse under his breath. "There is no difference in who I am now versus the man you were putting into his place a few moments ago."

"I don't think…"

He lifted his hand, silencing her. "You are a beautiful woman and I'm a man who is interested in getting to know you. That's all there is between us. Don't make more of this than what it is."

She relaxed slightly, but was still more than a little awestruck. "Your Highness, I can't…"

"You will call me Malik," he told her.

She shook her head. "I can't use your first name, Your Highness." She looked around again. "I have to go. I'm sure you have more important things to do."

He grabbed her hand before she could walk away. "Jina, don't leave. Just talk to me," he coaxed softly.

She started to shake her head again, glancing around because speaking to a world leader like this was a major breach in protocol. "I can't do this, Your Highness," she told him again.

He moved in closer, trapping her body with his against the table but not allowing any of the other guests to notice. "Here's what's going to happen, my blue eyed beauty," he told her in a soft but very firm voice. "You're going to walk out of here on my arm. I will treat you as if you are working for me as a translator or I can drag you out of here and treat you like an angry lover. The choice is yours."

Her eyes narrowed as he issued that threat. "You wouldn't!" she gritted out, furious now that he was talking to her like this.

His eyes moved over her lovely features, noting the angry color on her high cheekbones. "Oh, my pretty woman. You'd be surprised at what I dare. So which is it? With dignity or with derision? What is your choice?"

Her chin jutted out with his ultimatum. "You're not going to do this to me, Your Highness." His title was said with the highest degree of sarcasm that she could muster through her nervousness.

He chuckled. "Oh, I'm going to do this. We're going to leave here where you are self-conscious because you are surrounded by your colleagues and potential clients, and we're going to go someplace more private. If only to have a glass of wine together, we're going to talk and relax. And you're going to trust me."

Her mouth fell open with that comment. "You really expect me to trust you after you just threatened my career and my credibility?" she asked in astonishment, pretending that she wasn't trembling in anticipation from his words.

He smiled. "We're leaving."

She thought he was saying that to her but she realized that his comment was actually to the bodyguards who suddenly appeared in her line of vision.

Where they'd been before this moment, she had no idea. But before she could stop him, he was leading her out of the room. He stopped occasionally to speak with one or two of the lingering guests, making their departure look like a simple casual conversation. He turned to say something to one of his guards and Jina shook her head when she translated the message. She only knew a few words of Arabic but she knew enough so that she understood his command. "He can't get into the employee lockers," she explained. But the guard disappeared, off to get her personal belongings.

Jina was able to maintain her nervous anger almost the whole walk through the room. But when she saw the limousine waiting at the door for him, she pulled back.

Malik turned back to face the fascinating woman. "What's wrong?" he asked softly, turning so that she couldn't see his bodyguards.

Her eyes snapped from the vehicle, then up to his eyes, then back again. "I can't do this! I can't get into that vehicle! I mean, why would you want me to anyway? The only reason would be for..." she shook her head and pushed a stray lock of hair back behind her ear. "I'm not like that. I can't do it. I just..."

Malik used the expedient method of stopping her tirade by simply kissing her. Initially, she was too stunned to react but it took perhaps three seconds before he felt her lips soften, her body melt into his. His hands on her shoulders slid lower, wrapping around her waist and pulling her against his hardness. Malik was used to the softness of women, loved their smells and their figures, finding all the different shapes of women a turn on. But when this lovely, nervous, shy woman melted in his arms, the lust that surged through him was hard and fast. Never before had his mind left him so quickly.

The horns blasting startled him and Malik lifted his head. As he stared down into her soft, blue eyes, he realized that he needed to get them out of there quickly. She looked like he felt and the desire surging through him with that knowledge was powerful.

"Come with me," he growled, taking her hand and pulling her towards the limousine. They were inside the dark interior with the doors closed before her eyes cleared of the desire. He knew that he'd put that desire there and he could barely suppress his need as that reality hit him.

She was so lovely with her swollen lips and the confusion in those pretty blue eyes. But a moment later, the vehicle moved and the wariness returned.

"No, Jina," he told her softly. "I'm not going to spirit you away to some horrible, dark dungeon. We're going to my hotel and we'll have a glass of wine. We'll talk and have some food since you didn't eat enough earlier. And then I will ensure that you are home, in your own bed and," he smiled slightly, "alone." When she still looked anxious, he sighed. "I'll have you home and in your own bed by midnight. Will that suffice? Since it is Saturday night, I'm guessing you don't have a heavy work load tomorrow, is that correct?"

Her lips compressed as she thought about his offer. Was she bargaining with the devil? Was she a fool to listen to him and accept his proposition? Was she too trusting?

Of course she was! But was she going to do anything about it?

"Your Highness…"

"Malik. Say my name, Jina," he commanded gently, lifting his hand to touch her cheek.

She started to shake her head, not feeling comfortable enough to use his first name. He was a sheik! He was ruler of one of the most powerful countries in the world!

"I…"

His thumb caressed her lower lip, causing the skin to tingle, a bit like it was on fire. "Just say my name, Jina. It's an easy enough request. It won't hurt, no one is around who could admonish you so there is no breach in protocol. And I promise you, none of my bodyguards would care, or even know, that you were so familiar with me."

She laughed at that, unable to hide her amusement once again. "I'm sure there are very few people you allow to call you by your given name."

"That's true." He thought for a moment before he said, "What if I told you that there are about five people who would call me worse? And to my face?" He saw the surprise in her eyes. "And what's more, four of them are men I highly respect and they still try and take me down whenever they have the chance." When she looked at him doubtfully, he continued, "Okay, so they don't physically fight with me anymore. But there were days when it was all our headmaster could do to keep us from killing each other. It was only one blond haired brat that stopped all of it. And she still tries to interfere in our lives." He shifted slightly. "One night, she was so scared from a horror movie that she snuck into with us that she made me sleep on the floor underneath the window, just to make sure that the monsters wouldn't get in."

"No way," Jina replied, not believing him for a moment.

"Believe it," he assured her. "And I think I had to sleep there for several nights."

Jina shook her head. He was teasing her but it was working. She leaned back against the soft leather seat.

"It's true," he told her. "In fact, she's the only reason I don't have more broken bones."

"What do you mean?"

He leaned back and took her hand, playing with her fingers as he examined her nails. They were smooth and short. A worker's hands, he thought. "Scarlett was a five year old little tyrant who arrived at the boarding school. All of us basically hated each other but there were five of us that took that hatred to a new level. For about a year, there wasn't a day that passed when one or all five of us were throwing punches. I think I lived with a broken rib, not always the same one, for about six months of that year." He thought back to those days, shaking his head. "When that little tyrant showed up, all she had to do was put a hand on our arm or our shoulder and," he shrugged, not really understanding it either. "Well, we just stopped." He looked at her. "Now those men and Scarlett are my best friends. And besides you, they are the only ones that are allowed to call me by my first name."

"That's a sweet story," she said, not really believing him but thinking it was kind of him to try and make her feel more comfortable. "Where are we going?"

"To my hotel. I will order a bottle of wine and tempt you with one of the chef's amazing desserts."

The trembling increased and her eyes widened in fear and…yes…desire. Curiosity. "I don't want anything," she told him, wary of being alone with him.

"Fine, you'll have a cup of coffee with me and we'll talk. I'll let you ask me anything you want to know about me as a person and then you'll feel more comfortable."

She shook her head. "I doubt I'll feel comfortable with you alone in your hotel."

He shrugged his shoulder. "Then we will go to your apartment." He didn't wait for her to respond before he picked up a phone and issued a command in a language she didn't understand. A moment later, before Jina could even reply to his change of plans, the limousine was turning and heading out of Manhattan.

"We can't go to my apartment!" she gasped out, sitting up a bit straighter because they were dangerously close to her building.

He simply smiled slightly, not responding. Before she could form a coherent argument, the limousine was gliding smoothly to a halt in front of her building and Malik was getting out. He turned and offered his hand.

Jina stared at that hand, knowing she should be polite and accept his help but she also remembered the heat that seeped into her body every time she touched this man. Even inadvertent touches made her senses become inflamed.

In the end, she put her hand in his, but only for a moment. She couldn't endure much more.

She warily led him up the stairs and was painfully conscious of him right behind her. She was wearing only the black cocktail dress and it felt strange to know that he was right behind her, looking at her bottom.

She was hugely relieved when she reached her floor and she could move to the side. But the look in his eyes told her that he knew exactly what was going on inside her head.

"Are you laughing at me?" she demanded as soon as her door was unlocked. But she stood in the doorway, glaring up at him.

He chuckled softly and pressed her against the doorframe. "Laughing? No. Enjoying your...shyness?" He lifted a finger, running it along her neck. "Yes. I am enjoying your shy nervousness."

"I'm neither shy nor nervous," she lied, trying to appear sophisticated and unconcerned with having this large man inside her personal space.

His eyes moved over her features, noting the color that appeared. "Yes, you are. But I like it. You are refreshing."

Jina's lips curled into a grimace. "Refreshing. I'm not sure I like that adjective but," she shrugged, knowing there wasn't anything she could do. "I'm not shy though. I speak with people all day long. People I've never met before and I'm not bothered by introducing myself."

He gently pulled her down the short, dark hallway to her kitchen. "You're shy with me. And I like it. Because I know that you're nervous about being alone with me."

She wasn't going to argue with him on that point. But nor was she going to correct him. She wasn't nervous. That was such a tame description for what she was feeling. She was terrified. She could feel her heart beating wildly in her chest and her skin felt almost tingly and he wasn't even touching her at the moment.

He stepped back and saw the colorfully wrapped box sitting in her tote bag. "Are these the shoes that someone delivered to you?" he asked, lifting the box out of her bag. He pulled the box out and separated the tissue paper, lifting one perfect shoe out of the box and examining it. "They look lovely." His eyes moved to hers. "Why won't you wear them?"

She pursed her lips. "Because they are outrageously expensive. You'll have to take them back. I can't accept a gift like that."

He shrugged one massive shoulder. "I don't know how much they cost, but someone must have noticed how beautiful your legs are and wanted to give you a present to display them."

Jina looked at his fingers as they smoothed over the lines of the shoe. Even the red sole looked sensuous as his long fingers moved along the edge. Pulling her eyes away, she grabbed the tea kettle and turned to face the sink, away from that man's hands that she could so easily picture running along her body.

She couldn't believe how off-balance she felt, simply because this particular man was in her apartment and looking at a shoe.

She set the teapot down on a burner, then turned on the heat before turning back to face him. She felt somewhat back in control, but she should have just pushed him out of her apartment. Because this man was too large, too tall and too everything. He dwarfed her apartment, somehow even making the air seem more intense. That wasn't possible, was it? Air was air. It couldn't change forms simply because one man was in close proximity.

Very close proximity!

"What are you doing?" she demanded, suddenly realizing that he'd moved closer to her. She leaned against the countertop, trying to keep a couple of inches between them. Bad mistake! He lifted her up, his hands on her waist and easily set her down on the countertop.

He didn't respond to her question with words. His fingers slid down her leg and Jina said a silent thank you that she'd remembered to shave her legs this morning. Then he slipped her strappy sandal off of her foot, replacing it with the Louboutin pump.

"Perfect," he said, his head tilting back and forth as he looked at her leg. He then reached out and plucked the other shoe out of the box, repeating the process with her other foot.

That wouldn't have been such a problem, but the diabolical man somehow positioned himself between her legs, not giving her any space to close her knees primly together as she wanted to do. When he finished putting the shoe on her foot, he turned around, forcing her legs further apart, shocking her with his audacity and blatantly sexual moves.

"Now, what were you saying about not being nervous?" he asked a moment before his mouth covered her own. There was no chance to respond, not because he was kissing her but because he was really kissing her! Responding to his question was the furthest thing from her mind as his tongue invaded her mouth, teasing her and exploring her taste. When his teeth captured her lower lip, she gasped at the erotic feeling before he released it, kissing her again.

His hands were moving over her waist, sliding up and down her cocktail dress covered legs and hips. What she wasn't aware of was that he was sliding the material higher with each swish of his hands. Of course, she was fully aware when his hands grabbed hold of her hips and pulled her forward, causing her heat to cradle that hardness. But she couldn't be still. Not in this position. She didn't care that her skirt was up around her hips now or that his erection was pressing against her, making her body ache in places she'd never even known existed. All she knew, as she tilted her hips to get better contact, was that she wanted this man and she needed to shift against him. Unable to stop herself, she shifted again and again, moving so slightly in a desperate need to ease the ache that was centered low in her body.

The whistle on the tea kettle startled both of them. Jina looked up into his dark eyes, her mind not really understanding what he was doing to her. Or how he could do it so easily!

She pushed at his shoulders, relieved when he allowed her to push him back. Jumping down off of the countertop, she grabbed the tea kettle, lifting it off of the burner and turning off the heat. Her fingers were shaking when she reached up and took down two cups. When a strong hand took them out of her fingers, she sighed with relief. She suspected she'd drop them anyway. She was too rattled from the way he'd kissed her. And too shocked at how she'd responded! Good grief, the man knew how to kiss!

"Tea," she said softly and pulled down the tin that held all of her flavored teas. "What kind of tea would you like?" she asked.

"Any kind of tea is fine," he replied, watching her carefully. "Are you okay?"

Jina spun around to face him then leaned back. She hadn't been aware that he was so close. Again! She needed some space after that kiss!

Her eyes dropped to her hands, unable to maintain eye contact. "No. I don't think I'm fine."

"Talk to me Jina. Did I hurt you in some way?"

She shook her head. "Hurt me? No. You didn't hurt me in any way. But I have to ask why are you here?" She looked at his immaculate suit that probably cost as much as her entire year's rent money. "You're a sheik, Malik. What are you doing here? With me? It can't be simply because you enjoy our conversations because we haven't really talked about anything. So that really only leaves one reason. You want to have sex."

He was more than a little stunned by her directness, but he should have been prepared. "Yes," he replied honestly. "I want you. I've never denied that."

She lowered her lashes. "Yes, but you see, I don't...I can't..." she finally looked up into his eyes. "I can't be your mistress. And that's really all I could possibly be to you."

Malik didn't reply. He'd never really considered what the women in his life might think of his intentions. He'd never really thought about getting married, never having met a woman that he could stand talking with outside of the bedroom. Well, besides Scarlett, but she didn't really count. She wasn't a woman. He almost rolled his eyes. Of course, Scarlett was a woman but she was...well, she was like a kid sister.

He focused his dark eyes on her blue ones. "I'm going to make love to you, Jina. That's inevitable."

She sighed, trying to figure out why that bothered her so much. Her stomach tightened with anticipation, but there was something wrong about his absolute conviction.

"Malik," she forced his name out, "If you were just another man, this conversation would be different."

"How?" he demanded, not liking the idea of any other man touching her as he was going to touch her.

"If you were just an ordinary man, and there was this intense attraction between us, then I would risk an affair with you."

"At least you're willing to admit that there is an attraction," he replied, irritated still.

She smiled briefly. "Yes. I'll admit that much. But it can't go anywhere. And I have too much pride, too much at stake with my career, to risk just entering into an affair with a man like you. When I make love with a man, it is because I'm in love with him."

Malik understood her words. He didn't like what she was telling him, but he respected her even more because of her sentiments. "And have you ever been in love with a man?" he asked, his hands coming to pull the pins from her hair, massaging the scalp gently as he watched her eyes close with pleasure.

"No. I've never been in love with another man, Malik."

For some reason, her assurance helped ease the tension in his shoulders. This woman was a virgin, he realized. Yes, she might be lying to him. And this whole conversation might be a ruse to get him more interested in her. Women were diabolical creatures with amazing imaginations to get what they want. And many women wanted his ring on their finger and access to all of his wealth and the power that would be translated from him to his wife.

But he doubted that Jina was the kind of woman who would lie and cheat to get what she wanted. He sensed an innate honesty in her, a purity of spirit that he liked. A lot!

"Then we will become friends," he announced, pulling his hand away. Malik stepped back, his eyes lighting up with a special message that Jina didn't really understand. There was a triumphant depth to them, something that made her stomach muscles tighten in anticipation even worse than what she'd been feeling only moments before. How was it that he could be kissing her one moment and the next she felt the same intensity, but he wasn't even touching her?

"I'm not sure..." she started to say.

Malik interrupted her. "I completely understand and respect your wishes to not enter into a strictly sexual relationship. This will be a new adventure for both of us." He moved slightly closer, lifting his hand briefly to touch her cheek before pushing both of his hands into the pockets of his slacks. "I don't think that I've ever been friends with a woman. Especially a woman I want to make love to." The expression on his face indicated that he was just as surprised by his declaration as she was.

He leaned forward and gently kissed her on her cheek. "Sweet dreams, my beauty." A moment later he was gone.

Jina heard the door close on his exit but she didn't really understand what had just happened. He mentioned an adventure but what did he mean by that? What kind of adventure was he embarking upon?

Another shocking realization occurred to her. Malik was the kind of man that generated an enormous amount of energy wherever he was. While she was with him, she felt more alive than she'd ever felt in her entire life. Or at least more alive than she'd ever realized. With him gone, the exhaustion from being so alive seemed to overwhelm her. The tension dissipated and she felt like all of her bones were melting. Sinking into the sofa, she looked around and tried to understand why he could have such a strong impact on her.

Chapter 2

Jina stared at the message on her computer screen. This had to be some sort of mistake. It was impossible that he was the man who had hired her. Not only had he reserved her services for several short time periods, all of them adding up to a crazy twenty-four hours, he was paying her an outrageous sum of money! It was three times her normal hourly rate. No other client had ever paid that amount of money. Not for her services. Not only that, but the man hadn't specified exactly what she was going to be doing for him.

Normally a client would give the social or political event, any words to look out for, what their ultimate goal was, if they could, and she would research the various guests and venues so that she could be prepared and help her client move more easily among the others in the room. She also preferred to know which language she would be translating, but she was fluent in several, so she supposed she could wing it. As long as he understood that it was sometimes hard to shift from one language to another quickly.

Oh goodness, what could he be thinking? Why would he offer her such an outrageous sum of money? Did he think…?

No! Their last conversation together indicated that he would be more respectful of her wishes. That conversation had indicated that he was not going to do anything unsavory.

So why had he reserved her services for such an extraordinary amount of time? Most of her clients requested a two or three hour time frame. Sometimes longer if there was a big evening gala that was needed, but rarely longer than five hours. Twenty-four hours was unheard of!

Her cell phone rang even while she was holding it, still trying to figure out what this agency request meant. As it rang a second time, she knew exactly who was trying to reach her. It was him. She knew that it was Malik. She didn't even have to know his phone number, and there's no way that she could have because he hadn't given it to her. But this was him. Every cell in her body tightened with what she was describing to herself as fear, but she really knew that it was anticipation.

Was she going to answer it? She stared at the phone for a long moment, debating. He was now a client. She had to answer it! She couldn't simply ignore a phone call, especially after she'd received the news from her agency that this man had requested her services. But for 24 hours? How crazy was that?!

"Hello?" she answered as she lifted the cell phone to her ear, her fingers shaking.

"Good morning, beautiful," Malik's deep, sexy voice said through the airwaves. "Did you get the message from your agency?"

Jina took a deep breath and closed her eyes before she answered. "Yes, I received all the information." She was going to be perfectly professional about this, she told herself firmly. No personal problems, no silly qualms about the man and how incredibly handsome he was. She was going to treat him with courtesy and professionalism, just as she would any other client.

Letting her breath out slowly, she tried to calm down her racing nerves. "Can you give me a few more details about what kind of translation services you need?" Her free hand reached out, gripping the edge of the countertop as she waited for him to respond. Please, please don't say something horrible. For the past three nights, she had dreamed of this man and the way he made her feel when he'd kissed her that one time. She really didn't want to lose the fantasy of this man, because everything that she thought of him would go away as soon as he said something horrible. She tensed as she waited for his response, praying that he wasn't hiring her for services that she could not offer. Services that were illegal. No! He wasn't like that!

Was he?

Malik's deep voice broke through her anxiety. "The French Prime Minister is in town tonight and he has requested a meeting with me. I'm having dinner with him and several of his aides. I need you here tonight to help with translation services. Do you have anything to wear for an event like that?"

Jina let all of the air flow out of her in a whoosh. She was so relieved that he wasn't asking her to do something that she couldn't morally do. Not to mention, he was actually hiring her for a real, genuine job.

And then his words hit her. Not just any job either! He wanted help with the French Prime Minister! She'd never had such a high-level client before. Well, actually, Malik would be the client. But Jina knew that one client led to another client. If she could do a good job interpreting in front of the French Prime Minister and his aides, the French Embassy might hire her for additional jobs. Of course, each embassy and government had its own translation departments. There were people that were specifically trained in specific cultures and were cleared through their own governments.

The excitement that she was feeling at something so wonderful welled up inside of her and she had trouble speaking for a long moment. When she realized what was happening, she stammered out a response. "Of course! I would be more than happy to help you with any event tonight or in the future. The Prime Minister is a very nice gentleman, from what I hear." She took a breath, trying to calm down. She was rambling, and sounding a little bit too eager.

A moment later, a thought occurred to her. Was she eager for the job? Or was she eager to see Malik again? Either way, she felt more than a little silly. Her hand fluttered over her stomach as she tried to relax a little.

Malik's deep chuckle sent one of those crazy thrills through her body, making her heart pound so loudly that she was afraid he might be able to hear it through the phone. "I'll send over a dress for you anyway because I suspect you'll pull out yet another black dress and that simply won't do. Not for tonight. I think that you already have the shoes, don't you?"

Jina's cheeks turned a light shade of pink, and she was glad that he wasn't around to see it. That the deep chuckle that came across the phone told her that he knew exactly what was happening. "I have a dress, but I can't wear the shoes."

"If you're talking about the dress that you wore to that other event, I'm sending over something different. And if you don't wear the shoes, I will be very unhappy with you."

Jina laughed. "I'm not afraid of your displeasure," she said to him.

The soft murmur of his deep voice echoed in her ear once more. "Oh, I actually hope that you will disobey me. I'll take great pleasure in showing you exactly what happens to a beautiful woman who doesn't wear appropriate shoes." He hesitated for just a moment before he said, "Wear the black shoes, and let me see your beautiful legs ending with those shoes. Or I will put them on you just like I did the last time. If you aren't wearing them, I will consider that to be your requests for me to do exactly what I'm threatening."

Jina rolled her eyes. "That isn't a fair threat, Malik." She tapped her finger on the outside of the cell phone as she considered what she could say to change his mind. "It is unethical for me to accept a gift like that."

"Whoever sent those shoes must not be very concerned with ethics. I have no idea who sent to the shoes, but if you aren't wearing them on the ends of your very beautiful legs, I will put them on you. This is not a threat, my beauty. This is a promise."

After that, the line went dead.

She wanted to laugh but the man really was a bit too arrogant for her peace of mind. He thought he could get away with his trick but she wasn't as stupid as he probably thought she was.

But what could she really do about it?

Her eyes went to the bag with the beautiful shoes. They really would be perfect for dinner with the French Prime Minister, she thought.

Could she?

It would be extremely bad of her.

But the client demanded that she wear them.

Walking over to the box, she slid the shoes out and put them on one foot, extending her leg and tilting her foot back and forth, admiring the way her leg looked in the amazing shoe.

In the end, she couldn't resist the allure of an excellent pair of shoes. So she was standing in the shoes the following night when he knocked on her door. Not only that, she was wearing a beautiful new cocktail dress that had arrived by special messenger, she felt a bit flushed as the forest green dress hugged her figure and made her eyes pop with a bit more color.

She was completely unaware of the pink in her cheeks at the excitement of the night ahead. So when she opened the door, she smiled up at Malik as professionally as she could muster, grabbed her bag, her black evening wrap and walked out the door, unaware that Malik was standing in her doorway in stunned silence.

Malik watched the woman walk by him, his body hardening with each step she took. It was as if each step was a challenge, a dare for him to make love to her. It wasn't because of the shoes, although they did make her legs look...incredible!

No, there was something about her, something different in the way she was walking. There was a confidence about her that hadn't been there before.

When she looked over her shoulder, her pretty, blue eyes tossing out a silent challenge, he almost groaned with acceptance of that challenge. Oh yes, my beauty. You think you're in charge? Don't even try it!

A moment later, he was following her down the steps of her building. She was about to swish her black wrap around her shoulders but he took it out of her hands, lifting it up himself and holding it out for her. His eyes watched her as she realized she would actually have to step into his arms for the wrap to go around her.

Slowly, as if she wasn't quite sure what might happen if she accepted his dare, she turned around and allowed him to lay the material over her soft, white shoulders.

Malik wrapped the softness around her and then twisted the material so that she was facing him once more. As he draped the ends of the pashmina over her shoulders, he allowed the backs of his hands to touch her breasts, fully aware of the way her breath caught in the back of her throat.

Trembling from the shocking impact of his touch, Jina carefully laid her hand on Malik's outstretched arm, her fingers already shaking just from the slight contact. Had he done that on purpose? She looked up at him as the chauffer opened the limousine door for both of them. The look in his eyes told her without doubt that he definitely had done that on purpose.

And he was going to do it again at the first opportunity.

She should be offended. This was a business meeting, after all.

But in reality, her body was thrumming along after that touch and the admonishing words simply wouldn't form on her lips. And the thought, "Again," kept popping into her mind.

She looked down, realized that she was clenching her hands into fists on her lap. Trying to relax, she stretched her hands out carefully, not wanting him to be aware of her tension.

His deep chuckle told her that her efforts were pointless. The man saw everything!

"What have you done today?" he asked.

Jina took a deep breath but even that was a mistake. The effort only brought his scent to her nose. And boy! It was a wonderful scent! Musky, spicy and all male. She'd never thought that men smelled particularly nice or bad. There had been the boys in high school who had smelled like sweat. Normally, it wasn't such a bad smell but it wasn't particularly pleasant either. Oh, and there had been that horrible deodorant that the guys in high school and college thought smelled so great. It actually made her stomach clench in revulsion. Unfortunately, the boys hadn't ever caught on to how much the girls hated the smell.

This man's scent though? It was almost…sexual! It stimulated parts of her that she'd never known existed and she shifted in the soft leather seat, trying to ease the slight ache that was centered low in her pelvis.

"That's not going to help," he said softly beside her.

His deep voice sent shivers throughout her body. "What's not going to help?" she asked, her voice raspy and sounded strange to her ears.

"The shifting and trying to pretend that it isn't there."

"I don't know what you're talking about," she responded nervously. But she did! Goodness, she knew exactly what was happening between them. She'd read it in stories but hadn't ever experienced it before.

He didn't really answer her. He simply took her hand, ignoring her slight resistance as he laid the back of her hand flat against his rock hard thigh. Spreading her fingers out, she watched in tightening fascination as his finger stroked her palm. Up and down, over and back. When her fingers curled up, he simply smoothed them flat again.

"It's there. And it is stronger than the two of us."

She couldn't pretend any longer. It was just too much with his fingers stroking her hand and his closeness in the darkened interior of the limousine. "We have to resist it." No use trying to deny it any longer. It was shockingly obvious that there was something between them. What that really was, and what this man seemed to think would happen, she wasn't completely sure. All she was sure about was that this man was dangerous and what she was feeling was terrifying. It had to be resisted, no matter what.

"At least you are no longer pretending that it isn't there."

She tried to pull her hand away but his fingers tightened on hers. "I'm not done yet."

"We shouldn't be touching."

He chuckled softly. "Oh, Jina-love. We're going to be touching," he said softly while his fingers moved down the palm of her hand, up her bare forearm, "And so much more before tonight is over."

Her eyes had been watching his fingers, mesmerized by the way his long, tanned fingers looked against her pale skin. She'd never thought that she was particularly pale, but compared to his skin, she was almost luminescent.

"Stop," she whispered.

He shook his head. "I'm not going to stop," he countered.

Thankfully, the limousine came to a halt at that moment and she breathed a sigh of relief. Malik smiled triumphantly at her expression. "You think that this is a reprieve?" he teased.

Stepping out of the vehicle, he reached down and took her hand, helping her out. "It is not." His lips were close to her neck, brushing erotically against the shell of her ear and creating an intimacy with his body that was even more intense than what she'd endured in the limousine.

Jina looked up at the impressive French Embassy, her mind trying to focus on work but all she could think about was this man's touch on her overly sensitive skin. She wanted to pull her hand away, but he wouldn't let her.

As he led her through the doors, she was fully prepared to undergo a thorough security search. But they were greeted by the French Prime Minister himself as soon as the guards opened the door.

From that moment forward, the dinner was nothing like she had expected. First of all, Malik spoke French fluently. His accent was perfect, his understanding of even the most delicate innuendos swift. She quickly realized that there was no need for her to be here in an official capacity. She tried hard to stay angry with Malik about the trick, but her mind couldn't really work up the emotion. Unfortunately, she was still overwhelmed with his presence, with the amazing scent of the man and overawed by how handsome he looked in the tuxedo, not to mention, his brilliance at dealing with the prime minister who was subtly asking for several price cuts on oil deliveries.

The evening wasn't long, thankfully. But it was hard to concentrate when she was constantly sitting next to Malik or being touched by his hand, his arm. Even during dinner, he was there, sitting across the table from her and looking into her eyes. She could see the silent messages and couldn't stop the blushes from forming on her cheeks.

By the time they were saying their goodbyes to the prime minister and his wife, she wanted to just run home and protect herself. But there was still the drive back to her apartment. In a dark, intimate limousine.

From the moment the door closed on the embassy, she knew that she was in trouble. She could feel the air start to tingle with anticipation. When he held her hand, helping her into the limousine, she paused, looking up into his eyes. "You're taking me home, right?" she asked.

Malik hesitated for a moment. "If that's what you want," he told her.

Jina's mouth opened to affirm that she wanted to go home. But the words wouldn't come. All evening, she'd been tempted by him, by the subtle touches and loved the way he smelled. She wanted to move closer, let her nose inhale his scent right at the edge of his starched, white collar. But that would be too forward. Too brazen.

Her hesitation caused Malik's eyes to flare and she shook her head. "No Malik. I don't..." she started to say something but he bent down and kissed her, right there in front of the French Embassy!

And she reacted the way she always did when he touched her in any way. Her mind froze and her body trembled. But even worse, this time, she moved closer to him, wanting to feel his hard chest against her soft breasts. Wanting to know what it would be like to be embraced by this man.

He lifted his lips after only a few moments, the fire in his eyes heating her from the inside out. Instead of saying anything, knowing she should tell him no but unable to make her lips form the words, she ducked into the limousine.

He followed quickly and the vehicle moved off smoothly even as the tension inside the back increased.

"You're quite beautiful," he told her.

Jina looked down at her hands that were clenching her small evening purse on her lap.

"Malik, this isn't...I'm not really..."

"You're not comfortable with where this is going," he stated calmly. "Where do you think this is going?" he asked.

She looked straight ahead and debated how to answer his question. "I think we're...going to your bed."

Malik looked at the gentle beauty that appeared both terrified and excited. And that aroused him even more. "Is that a bad thing?" he asked, taking one of her hands and spreading the fingers out.

She looked up into his eyes, blue against black, soft against hard. "I don't want it to happen, Malik," she whispered through lips that were numb with the confusion running through her.

"You know that it is inevitable, right?" he asked.

She thought about denying it but she couldn't. Ever since the moment their eyes had clashed…goodness, had it only been three days ago? Yes, she'd known from that moment that this would happen. Perhaps not consciously. She'd been irritated with him then. But from the moment he'd kissed her in her apartment, she'd known that their paths would come to this point. "I don't want it to happen," she reiterated. "This isn't who I am. I don't…" she sighed. "I don't sleep around."

"I never thought you did."

She looked down at their hands, once again intertwined. "I know that…" she forced her mind to work. "I know that you are the type of man who…can coax me into your bed. And I'm sure…"

He waited, wondering where this was going. "What are you sure about?" he asked gently. The more he watched her, watched the emotions run through her eyes, the more he wanted her. She was like a beautiful, refreshing stream with those blue eyes telling him everything she was feeling. And her long, dark lashes fluttered around her eyes, making her skin look extra pale by comparison. He longed to run his fingers through her lush, dark hair and feel the silken texture. But he wanted her to be with him the whole way.

He sighed and lifted her hand to his mouth, his teeth and lips nibbling along her wrist and he almost smiled when she gasped at the desire he knew she was feeling.

"Here is what is going to happen," he started out and he could sense her holding her breath. "I will take you back to your apartment tonight." Malik felt her fingers relax slightly and he smiled even as he wished she were a bit less…innocent. No, he corrected himself. It excited him that this particular woman had never been with another man before. She was his. Every delectable inch of her would be his woman. It would just take a bit more time before he could finalize their union.

"Thank you."

Malik shook his head. "Oh, you are not getting away from me so easily," he replied, then almost laughed out loud with relief when he saw the eagerness in those lovely, blue eyes. "Here is what we can do. I can see that you are not opposed to being with me." He ran a finger over the shell of her ear, suppressing a smile when he felt her shiver. "May I venture a guess that you are opposed to our union on such short acquaintance?"

Jina considered his comment. "I don't know what it is about you, Malik, but yes. I am not comfortable sleeping with someone that I've known for only a few hours."

He smiled slightly. "Ah, my beauty, there will be very little sleeping when we come together. And I can assure you, that I don't want you feeling comfortable around me. That's the very last thing I want when you are with me."

She shifted against him on the leather seat, her leg accidentally brushing against his hard thigh but the movement caused things inside of her to tighten in a strange way. "I don't think we're…"

He stopped her by kissing her lips, his mouth demanding more from her than she'd thought possible to give but the way he was kissing her made her want to give it to him. There was just something about this man that compelled her, drove her harder, needing him in an elemental way.

When he lifted his head, he was looking directly into her startled blue eyes. "Don't even consider that we won't be together, Jina. We will. The timing of our relationship is all we need to negotiate."

She shook her head, not liking his words but he interrupted her. "I have to go back to Sarkit tomorrow," he explained. "I will need your services when I return. You will help me?" he asked.

Jina considered his words. It would be better for her if she turned down the assignment. It would be safer. For her at least. But instead of telling him no, which she knew in her head she should do, she agreed. "Yes. I'll help you," she replied. "But you speak perfect French, Malik. You don't need my translation services. Call my agency and cancel the order. I won't take money from you."

He laughed softly. "I won't do it. I want you by my side."

She shifted again, having forgotten the surge of lust that sprang through her body when she did that and she gripped his shoulders as her body slowly settled back down. "I need to have this conversation while not seated on your lap, Malik."

His hands continued to hold her hips, his fingers lightly moving against the curve of her bottom. "I think this conversation is going extremely well with you right here."

She would have laughed at his arrogance, but his hand shifted and she was painfully aware of his hands on her hips, the heat coming to her skin from his fingers and the crazy sensations those fingers created inside of her.

She wanted to…No! She couldn't do that! It was wrong and very, very dangerous!

"Malik, I don't think…"

And he kissed her again, his lips coercing her into kissing him back once again. Only when she was clinging to him did he finally lift his head and look down at her once again.

"You were saying?"

She blinked, not sure what she was saying any longer. She wasn't even sure what she was thinking. "Um…"

He smiled slightly. "You were saying that you will accompany me as a translator next Friday night."

She opened her mouth to argue with him, but he shook his head, his eyes warning her that he would only repeat the kiss if she decided to argue with him. "You're not playing fair," she laughed, leaning back but he wouldn't let her escape his lap.

"No. I never play fair. I play to win."

Her laughter disappeared and she stared at his chin. "Malik, I'm not really in your league. Why me?"

He considered her words, not sure what she was asking. "You have to know that you are beautiful, Jina."

She shook her head. "Malik, I'm just like any other woman. There isn't anything special about me."

He couldn't believe she was saying such things. And, from the look in her eyes, she truly believed that she was simply an ordinary woman with ordinary looks. "Then you will have to trust me that you are special," he told her and kissed her, gently this time.

"Come," he told her when the vehicle came to a stop. "I will walk you to your door and you will tell me what you wear to sleep at night."

Jina was so shocked by his command, she couldn't stop the burst of laughter. "I certainly am not!" she told him with finality but she allowed him to lead her to her apartment door. When she pulled the keys out of her small bag, he took them from her and opened the door, putting a hand to the small of her back to guide her into the dimly lit interior of her apartment.

"What are you doing?" she asked, pressing herself against the wall as he passed by her.

Closing the door firmly, he looked down into her eyes. "Are you going to tell me what you sleep in at night?" he asked, his lips hovering above hers.

"Absolutely not," she told him, holding her breath as she waited for him to kiss her again.

He smiled again. "Then I'm going to find out, my pretty one. If you won't give me the information, I must discover the answer on my own." He paused for a moment as he bent lower. "And I'm very good at investigating," he promised.

Jina blinked when he simply walked away from her. His large form walked away, stepping through the only other door in the apartment. Her bedroom!

She quickly gathered her wits about herself and pushed away from the wall. "You can't go in there!" she gasped.

Malik ignored her and simply started opening her drawers. The first one contained her underwear and Malik looked inside. Jina had no idea what might be going through his mind but he shook his head. "No. This simply won't do," he told her as one tanned finger lifted a pair of white, cotton underwear into the air. "I need to think of you wearing lace," he said, his eyes moving to her breasts as if he could see through the material of her gown. "Red lace." He tilted his head slightly. "No. Black lace." With that, he nodded his head and shut the drawer. "I'll fix that for you."

Jina had no idea what he meant by that, but she grabbed her underwear from his fingers, pushed it back into her drawer and closed it with a snap. "My underwear is fine," she told him firmly.

"No. It isn't," he countered with a chuckle. But instead of arguing with her further, he opened another drawer and found her pajamas. "Ah! This is what I've been looking for," he told her and, before she could stop him, he'd pulled out a long, flannel nightgown that had definitely seen better days. "What is this?" he demanded.

Jina couldn't believe how ugly the thing looked in his hands. "Please, Malik. Just leave it alone." She'd hated that thing for years, but since no one ever saw her in her ridiculous, old-fashioned nightgowns, she'd never bothered to get new ones. Besides, they kept her warm during the winter! She hated being cold. It got down into her bones and made her ache with the pain. Flannel was warm. Flannel kept her warm! She even had flannel sheets for the winter along with several blankets that she buried herself under as soon as a chill hit the air.

She tried to pull it out of his hands, but he whipped it away so that he could examine it closer. "Please tell me this isn't what you actually wear, my beautiful woman," he asked as he looked down into blue eyes that were glaring up at him. "I can't believe a woman with your sensuality would wear this."

Those words stunned her and she froze, her mouth hanging open for a long moment. She shook her head. "I never felt sensuous until…" she realized what she was about to reveal and stopped herself. But he caught it anyway and smiled.

"That's good." Then he turned back to the drawer, pulling out another long, flannel nightgown. "But this is not. I will fix this as well," he announced. He dropped both nightgowns back into the drawer, then pulled her into his arms. "I will imagine you draped in silks and satins, Jina. And lace underneath all of your prim dresses." He bent down and kissed her neck, nibbled on her ear. "I will also imagine peeling back those prim layers myself so that I can view the sight underneath. I can already picture your pink nipples peeking through a black lace corset with a red bow right," he pressed his finger between her breasts, "here," he told her with a slow, wicked smile as he nipped her lower lip.

Jina was having trouble breathing, picturing exactly what he was saying too vividly in her imagination. "I won't wear them," she told him.

His smile widened with her defiance. "You will. You will wear them for me, won't you?"

She shook her head but he chuckled, sending yet another thrill through her body and making that place between her legs ache with an unprecedented need.

He didn't wait for an answer, bending lower and taking her lips in a soul-drugging kiss that left her clinging to him. But when it was over, he lifted his head and stepped back. "Until Friday night," and, a moment later, he was gone.

Jina looked around, startled to find herself alone in her bedroom. Alone in her apartment. And all of the air particles slowly started to fizzle out and the excitement that was always around when Malik was here, settled to a low, steady throb.

Chapter 3

A month later, Jina was a basket case. Malik flew into New York City, sometimes for just one night and sometimes for a whole weekend. They had dinner together every time he flew into town and on those precious moments when they had a whole weekend together, she delighted in walking through Central Park, going to the zoo, showing him all the silly, tourist sites in New York City. Or he would take her by helicopter to a house far in the mountains and they would spend their time talking, cooking, eating and exploring both the trails and each other.

He never took the physical aspect of their relationship all the way though. When she asked him to stop, he immediately stopped. She had no idea how hard it was for him, but their time together was just about killing her. Every time, he got a little further before the sensuality of their caresses became too much.

She stood in front of the mirror tonight, smoothing the red silk of her dress down over her hips and trying to take in deep, cleansing breaths, hoping that it would stop the trembling in her hands. Well, in her whole body.

Tonight, she wasn't going to ask him to stop. She'd had four days away from Malik and she'd done some soul searching over those four days. Jina realized that Malik wasn't her happily ever after, but he was the man of her dreams and she should grab hold of whatever time they had together and enjoy it. She wasn't going to be afraid of what he could make her feel any longer. Tonight, she was going to find out what all the fuss was about.

It had been difficult to decide which pretty underthings she would wear for the big event. Beautifully wrapped boxes arrived almost daily with lingerie, satin nightgowns, silk robes, beautiful shoes not to mention chocolates, amazing coffee or small treats. She was getting odd looks from the other residents in the building because of all of the boxes that arrived daily.

And tonight, she was wearing one of those presents. Well, two, actually. The bra and panty set made her feel incredibly feminine. Right at this moment, all she wanted to do was to open the door and tear off her clothes so that Malik could see her in this set. It looked amazing on her, transforming her body almost from a demure, prim librarian to an exotic creature, ready for pleasure. And that is exactly what she was tonight. She was ready. She was exotic. She wanted pleasure and she wasn't going to allow any doubts or misgivings to get in the way of making love with Malik tonight.

When the doorbell rang, her trembling increased but she forced her feet to carry her to the door. Opening the door, she peered around the side, her stomach clenching when she saw Malik standing just outside.

Malik took in the red dress which looked fabulous on Jina, but what truly caught his glance was the look in her eyes. Peering down into those blue eyes, he knew that tonight, he would be holding this woman in his arms. There was just something different and he wanted to lift her into his arms and make love to her right here, but he also wanted to savor the anticipation.

It had been over a month in this woman's company. Never had he waited this long to have a woman but he didn't care. He instinctively knew that she would be worth every second of the wait.

"You're mine tonight, aren't you?"

Jina's mouth fell open in shock. "How did you...I mean...what...?"

Malik laughed softly and stepped into the apartment, closing the door softly behind him. When they were alone, he looked down into her worried blue eyes and knew that she had given in. Pressing her backwards, he didn't relent until she was pressed against the wall. Taking her hands, he lifted them above her head even while his mouth captured hers and his knee pressed between her legs.

Jina was shocked when he pressed against her like this. She'd never experienced anything so erotic as this moment, this man pressing against her in this way. She felt both defenseless and powerful at the same time. Instinctively, she pressed her curves against his chest, thrilling at the way he groaned, deepening the kiss.

When he lifted his head, she stared up at him. "How did you...?"

"It was in your eyes, love," he told her. Stepping back, he continued to hold her hands with his long fingers. "Come. We'll have dinner."

She wasn't sure she wanted dinner and held back slightly. She really wasn't in the mood to eat.

When he looked back down at her, one hand on the door and one hand holding onto hers, he felt her hesitation. When he noticed the heat in her eyes, he smiled to reassure her. "Oh yes, we're going to consummate this relationship tonight. Never fear," he told her and nibbled against her lips. "But we will do so on my terms. We will dine and you will tell me about your week."

She rolled her eyes at his commands but he didn't relent. He did take her out to a restaurant, but she was too caught up in their plans for the evening to really eat anything. And the small bites that she did consume, she didn't taste because Malik was sitting across from her and she knew what was going to happen.

When he settled her back into the limousine, he called out a command to his driver and they were off.

"Where are we going now?" she asked, praying silently that he didn't have tickets to some concert or ballet or theatre. All she wanted was to be alone with him.

"I agree, love," he said and pulled her into his arms. He kissed her until she was whimpering with need, not sure what to do or how to move to assuage this need.

The limousine pulled up outside of the St. Regis Hotel and Malik exited before extending his hand to Jina. The guards were already surrounding them but she had eyes only for this man.

When they were in the private elevator, he looked down into her eyes. "Are you sure?" he asked, his hands lightly resting on her waist but she could feel the tension, knew that he could feel it as well.

"I'm sure," she whispered back, looking up at him so that he knew that she was clear about what would happen tonight. "Thank you for waiting so long. But tonight, I'm very sure that I want to experience bliss in your arms." And with that, she lifted herself higher, pressing her breasts against his chest while she kissed his jaw.

That wasn't enough for him but he held still. Only until the elevator doors opened once again and he took her hand, leading her down a long hallway.

When he stopped in front of a double set of doors, he turned back to her, looking into her blue eyes. "I can't tell you how painful this wait has been for me, my beauty," he said and tugged her gently into the suite, closing the doors behind him.

All night, Jina had been waiting for this to happen. But now that she was here, in his bedroom with him towering over her like this, she was nervous. She looked around, trying to take in the extravagance of the suite but she was too focused on Malik and the way he was prowling the room.

"How about a glass of wine?" he suggested.

Jina looked up at him, startled. "Wine?" Weren't they going to make love? Wasn't he going to…take her into his arms and…well, carry her off to the bed or something?

Malik laughed softly at the confused expression in her eyes. "Yes. We will get there," he promised her. "But first, we will have dinner. And wine. And you will relax."

Jina's fingers tightened around her purse. "I'm relaxed," she announced, nodding her head to reinforce her words. She wasn't relaxed in any way!

His smile told her that he didn't believe her. Not even a little bit. Moved behind a bar, he pulled out two glasses, pouring some wine into both then walking over to hand her one. "To the night," he told her and clinked glasses with her.

Jina took a sip of the wine but she couldn't taste anything. She was too nervous. She wanted to get this over with, to be in his arms. She'd waited so long and pulled back so many times and this was the night. She didn't want to wait. She didn't want to relax!

"Malik…" she started to say but he shook his head. "Dinner."

Jina sighed and took a long swallow of her wine. "Dinner," she repeated with resignation.

Looking over at Malik, she watched with fascination as he lifted the phone and told someone to bring dinner to the suite. Her eyes were captured by his lips, by the way he looked over at her and those dark eyes made her stomach tighten. Anticipation was throbbing inside of her and she smiled slightly.

Dinner? He wanted to wait for dinner?

She mentally shook her head. She wasn't hungry for food. And she was relatively sure that she wouldn't be able to eat anything, much less taste it. So ordering an expensive meal for them was pointless.

Besides, he was just teasing her. She could see it in his eyes and knew that he was trying to take control.

He could have control, she thought as she squared her shoulders. But she wasn't going to eat and she wasn't going to wait.

Setting her glass down on the table, she turned to face Malik who was still discussing dinner options. When her fingers moved to the tie on her waist, she knew that his eyes were following her movements. He'd stopped speaking, was just staring at her.

"Tell them we'll order later," she commanded, not sure where this newly assertive and definitely not shy woman had come from. Never before had she told a man what to do when it came to sex. Good grief, she'd never done anything even slightly sexual before. Kissing in high school and college, but that was as far as things went.

Until tonight.

Maybe there was just something about Malik. Or perhaps it was the night, her decision, the underwear she was wearing…

Whatever the reason, she wasn't waiting any longer to experience this man's lovemaking. Too many nights she'd lain awake wondering, her body throbbing with curiosity and need.

Tonight, she was going to find out everything.

She heard Malik's deep voice repeat her command and a moment later, he put the phone back down.

Leaning back against the sofa, he watched Jina as she fumbled with the tie of her wrap dress. She was nervous, but she was beautiful. She'd told him they would eat later, so they were going to eat later. And he was going to feast on this woman for a long, long time.

"I hope you had a snack before I picked you up," he told her as he pushed away from the sofa, walking towards her. "You're not going to be eating for a while."

Jina smiled slightly at that warning. She didn't really believe him, but nor did she care. He was finally coming towards her and her fingers trembled, both with anticipation and nerves.

"Keep going," he commanded, watching her carefully. She was adorable, he thought. Well, adorable in a sexy, beautiful, must-have-her kind of way.

Jina hesitated, her eyes unable to look away from him. Her fingers actually tangled in the knot, making it worse as she tried to get it undone. "I think I've made a mess of it," she finally told him, biting her lip with frustration. "I wanted to be all sexy and confident and simply drop my dress to entice you."

He smiled slightly, enchanted by her honesty. "Oh, you are enticing me, my dear," he told her and stepped closer, easily releasing the knot then stepping back again. "Proceed," he coaxed.

Jina held the material together, trying to regain that confidence that seemed to have suddenly evaporated. She took a deep breath and tried, she really did! But her hands just wouldn't pull the fabric away. She wished she was that confident, but…stripping down in front of this man was a bit more daring that she could handle.

Malik took pity on her and stepped closer once again. "You're a beautiful woman, Jina," he told her and took both of her hands, causing her to lose her grip on the dress. The sides fell open, revealing the lace underneath.

Jina looked up into his eyes as she felt the cold air hit her skin. When she heard his sharp intake of breath, she felt a resurgence of that illusory confidence. With shaking fingers, she pushed the material off of her shoulders, letting it drop to the floor.

Then she waited.

Malik didn't move. He couldn't. This woman was more beautiful than he'd thought possible. He'd felt all of her curves over the past several weeks, but the woman standing in front of him was more. So much more! Her breasts were full, straining against the material and her stomach curved softly before flaring out to full hips and long, long legs. How a woman who barely topped five feet, six inches could have legs that long, he had no clue. But at this point, he didn't care.

His eyes moved back up to her face, stopping at all the lovely female parts of her once again. "I agree. Dinner can wait."

A moment later, he lifted her into his arms and kissed her, making her toes curl with the erotic sensations. When her feet were once again touching the carpeting, his hands were free to move, sliding up her almost naked body and leaving a trail of fire in their wake.

While his mouth made love to hers, one of his fingers slid up her arm, hooking the strap of her lace bra and pulling it downward, revealing her breast to his hungry gaze.

She gasped when she felt his thumb flick her already hard nipple and pulled away, her fingers clutching at his shirt for support.

"Pink," he commented.

"What's pink?" she asked, breathing hard and trying to understand what was happening to her. She'd always been reserved but right at this moment, all she wanted to do was pull his clothes off and feel his bare chest against her body, to feel him move against her in the way that only he could do to her.

"Your nipples," he replied, then lifted her into his arms so that her breast was at the same level as his mouth and he captured the peak, taking it into his mouth, laving the sensitive skin and nipping it ever so slightly.

Jina hadn't ever felt sensations this intense before. Even when he'd been kissing her, his hands moving over her body over the past few weeks, she'd never felt this out of control.

"Malik!" she whimpered.

Slowly, he lowered her again but wouldn't give her up completely. Instead, he carried her through one of the doors to his bedroom, setting her down on the bed. She looked perfect there, he thought as he ripped his shirt off, then stripped off his pants.

"You're all mine tonight, Jina," he growled as he came back over her, pressing one of his knees between both of hers.

Jina's hands were still trembling, but she love the way he looked, all muscle and dark hair. "And you're mine," she whispered back. At least for tonight, she thought silently.

His mouth moved down her shoulder again, capturing her other nipple through the lace of her bra. When she was crying out and arching into his mouth, only then would he pull the material back with his teeth and lavish more attention on the nipple.

One finger smoothed down her stomach and he almost laughed at her indrawn breath. But he was in too much pain and loving every moment of this time with her. He wanted to take things slowly, but he wanted to ravish her as well, pound into her tight, hot flesh and make her his completely.

When his fingers slid inside of her, he had to close his eyes as he discovered how wet and incredibly tight she was. It wasn't enough though. He wanted it all. Moving lower, his lips kissed a path from her breast to her stomach, exploring there for several moments until he moved even further south. When he smelled her essence, he breathed her in, enjoying the amazing scent of her.

His fingers moved inside of her and he watched in fascination as she arched into his hand, moving her hips to get his hand in the place she wanted him to be. Malik tried to resist, wanting to watch her explode around his fingers. But she just smelled too good and he couldn't resist taking a taste. And then one small taste wasn't enough. His tongue moved against her sensitive flesh, making her squirm and scream at intervals even while his fingers continued to weave their magic.

And then it happened. Malik focused on that bud of nerves and felt her body climax around him, her body tightening around his fingers and her own hands diving into his hair while her hips tried to move away from his mouth.

Slowly, ever so slowly, he relaxed and allowed her to come down from that climax. He reached for protection as he loomed over her, his body aching as she shifted on the bed.

Malik couldn't hold back. Not any longer. Too much time he'd spent thinking about this moment and, now that it had arrived, it was much more incredible than he'd ever imagined.

Kissing his way back up her body, he moved so that his erection was poised at her opening. "Open your eyes, Jina," he told her softly.

When her pretty blue eyes were smiling up at him and her soft, pale hands were once again wrapped around his neck, he pressed into her, watching her eyes widen as he started to fill her up. Deeper and deeper he went, each thrust pressing more completely into her. He felt her barrier at the same time that he felt her legs wrap around his waist. In one swift move, he broke through and stilled, watching her beautiful features for any sign that he'd hurt her. But all he saw was the wonder in her eyes.

"So that's what it feels like," she whispered, amazed as she rubbed her legs against his hips and sides. "I think I like it," she told him.

Malik would have laughed if he weren't in physical pain from holding still. "Ah my love, this is only the beginning," he told her.

Jina had heard conversations around the employee locker rooms. Intercourse wasn't all that spectacular for most of the women who talked so she wasn't expecting anything more. In fact, she was bracing herself for a long wait while Malik came to the same beautiful pinnacle that he'd brought her to only moments ago.

But the first time he shifted inside of her, she knew that those women had been wrong! Oh goodness, had they been wrong!

Glancing up at Malik, she gripped his shoulders, worried now. "Malik?" she gasped when he pressed into her again, causing a spiral of sensations to whip through her body. Just like moments before, she could feel that building. With each thrust, that feeling intensified, made her both cringe and pull for it, wanting something, needing that crazy feeling again.

"I'm here, love," he promised and moved faster, shifting his hips and saw the way her eyes widened again. Then she arched into him, her head thrown back and she screamed out. Malik felt her nails against his skin while he watched. He was so close himself, but he wouldn't release his control until she'd climaxed again. Over and over he pounded into her tight sheath, one hand moving down, helping her out by pressing his thumb against that point where all sensation originated.

A moment later, she splintered apart, her body grabbing onto his and he pounded into her, finding his own release and holding her close, trying very hard to protect her even as the most incredible orgasm of his life took over his body.

A long time later, he lifted his head and looked down at Jina, worried that he was crushing her with his weight. Rolling over, he pulled her so that she was now on top of him. He wasn't willing to give up being as close as possible with her just yet.

"Are you okay?" he asked, pushing her hair out of her eyes.

Jina thought about that for a long moment. Was she okay? Her body had just gone through the most incredible experience of her life.

"I don't think that 'okay' describes what I'm feeling right now," she told him honestly, propping her chin on top of her stacked hands on his chest.

Malik's hands smoothed down her back, coming to a stop on her bottom. "How would you describe yourself at this moment?" he asked.

Jina looked up at the headboard, considering all the adjectives she could give him. "Hungry," she finally teased. "I can't believe we skipped dinner for…."

She yelped when he flung her over, right back on her back and loomed above her. "Would you care to try again?" he asked, his hand moving threateningly higher on her ribs.

Jina laughed, trying to wiggle away but he was much stronger than she was. And he was much better at tickling!

"Okay! Okay!" she begged, grabbing onto his hands and pulling his fingers away from her waist which was painfully ticklish. "I feel amazing," she finally said, her hands coming up to touch his cheek. "Thank you, Malik. That was wonderful. More than I could have imagined."

"Better," he told her as he bent to kiss her gently.

He stood up and walked into the bathroom, coming back out a moment later and picking up the phone. "But your every need must be satisfied," he told her.

Jina pulled the sheet over her nakedness, unable to just lie on the bed while his eyes moved over her. He had no qualms about being naked, she realized as he spoke to someone on the phone. He hung up the phone and turned back to look down at her.

"Where were we?" he asked, his eyes noticing that she was covering herself. "Seriously?" he teased and pulled the sheet lower. "Not happening, Jina," he told her and his mouth latched onto her nipple again. "Sheets only get in the way."

Jina closed her eyes as sensations swamped her all over again. "I thought dinner was on the way," she said, then gasped when his teeth nipped at her.

"It is."

"Shouldn't we..." she couldn't finish that question because he lifted her knee, sliding himself between her legs once again.

"Yes," he replied and moved closer. "We definitely should."

Jina would have laughed but...well, she couldn't do anything other than follow this man's lead. Again!

"I think I'm going to keep you," he said as he rolled over, pulling her legs so that she was straddling his hips.

"Right," she replied, balancing by placing both of her hands on his chest. Her fingers were restless though. They wanted to explore.

"I'm serious," Malik challenged. "You're mine, Jina. And I'm going to keep you."

Jina laughed even as she bent her head lower, kissing the middle of his chest.

"You think I'm kidding," he said while his hands moved her own hips lower on his. He grabbed another foil package and handed it to her. "Do the honors while I tell you how things are going to be."

Jina didn't care what he wanted to explain to her. She took the package and tore it open, then stared at the condom, trying to figure out how to get it on correctly. "I guess…" she started to say and slid the top of his erection on the ring. "Like this?" she asked, grabbing onto the shaft. "And do I…?" she pressed the material down, rolling it lower and lower. "I think I like this," she told him as she shifted against him. "A lot!"

Malik released a bark of laughter but he was too intent on his mission. "Right. It looks perfect to me," he told her but he didn't really care. He was too turned on by her soft hands against his erection. He had to be inside of her. Now!

"Come, my beauty," he said and lifted her up, impaling her on his erection and slowly lowering her down. He watched her face, being careful not to move too quickly. This was only her second time and he didn't want to hurt her again.

"Are you okay?" he asked.

Jina closed her eyes and shook her head. "Definitely not okay now," and she lifted her hips up, experimenting with various movements, trying to see which way felt the best. But with Malik, there really wasn't any wrong way to do this. Every way she moved, she felt full and incredible! This man, this moment…it was better than her dreams.

Malik couldn't believe how incredibly erotic his woman looked as she moved against his body. She was every man's fantasy come true. She was his fantasy in real life!

He reached up and cupped her breasts, tweaking her nipples as he watched her. And when he couldn't take the slow pace any longer, his hands moved lower, taking over the pace, listening to her sexy noises to determine how close she was.

Moving his hand lower, he helped her find that point and, when she shuddered over to her climax, he couldn't help but find his own because of the way she felt and the beauty of her body when she was in the throes of an orgasm. It was beauty personified!

Chapter 4

Jina should be exhausted. It was the middle of the night and her body was so tired, she wanted to sleep. But being curled up next to Malik, her mind wouldn't settle down.

After eating a delicious meal in bed with lots of wine and laughter, then making love again, she'd tried to get him to take her home.

"No. You're staying here with me," he told her and pushed their meal out of the bedroom door, then came back to bed with her. Turning off the light, he wrapped his arms around her as he pulled the sheet over her body.

Jina wiggled against him, trying to get closer. She loved him. It was a startling revelation, but she couldn't deny what she was feeling any longer.

In fact, she couldn't believe how much she loved him! It wasn't the sex, although she also couldn't believe how amazing it was with this man. No, the feelings she was experiencing were more about how he treated her, the gentle way he touched her…when they weren't in bed…the way he waited until she was ready and all of the sweet, kind ways that he showed her that he was a wonderful man.

Jina didn't delude herself into thinking that he felt the same way. Malik was a powerful, wealthy man and all of the gifts he'd sent, all of the trips and the ways he spoiled her…she suspected that someone else had arranged all of those surprises.

She didn't care. She loved this man and she was going to be with him for as long as she could.

Yes, it was going to hurt when he left her and moved on to the next woman. Possibly a lot! A smarter woman wouldn't have put herself into this position. A smarter woman would have run in the opposite direction when Malik walked into the room.

Jina sighed, knowing that she wasn't that smart woman.

"If you keep wiggling like that, you're not going to get any sleep," his deep voice warned.

Jina jerked slightly and looked up at him. He was wide awake! One arm propped behind his head, all of those delicious muscles flexing. She could see him clearly with the moonlight and the lights from the city since they hadn't closed the drapes over the windows. But there was no noise other than the sound of their breathing.

Lifting herself up, she turned slightly so that she could see him. Unfortunately, that meant she wasn't fully wrapped around him any longer and she felt cold without his heat.

"No. That's not going to work," he told her and rolled over so that she was once more in his arms and their bodies touching as much as possible. "What's on your mind?" he asked even as his fingers moved along her body.

Jina's hand grabbed those tantalizing fingers. "Nothing important," she lied.

Malik looked down into her eyes and knew that, whatever had been going on inside her beautiful mind, it had been very important. As had his own thoughts. "You're going to have to marry me, you know," he commented. He'd been tossing that idea over in his mind for the past week. Tonight had only solidified his decision that he had to marry this woman. He couldn't seem to think without her close by so his only solution was to bring her to Sarkit and love her like this every night, for the rest of their lives.

Jina's body froze with his words, but she forced her muscles to relax. He was only teasing her, she told herself. It wasn't truly a marriage proposal. "That would be nice," she told him, lifting her hands so that her fingers could dive into his hair. It was so thick and felt silky against her fingers. She loved his hair! Goodness, she loved everything about this man. She'd even gotten used to his arrogance. That thought made her laugh.

"What's so funny?" he asked, bending down and capturing her nipple in his mouth.

Jina gasped at the unexpected pleasure. It was so intense, she couldn't seem to answer him.

Malik lifted his head but his thumbs and fingers took over. "Tell me what you were thinking about, Jina," he commanded.

Jina shook her head, her hands coming out of his hair to slap his hands still. "I can't think with you doing things like that to me," she told him.

Malik laughed softly. "Good. That was my intention. I want to know the truth. You kept tensing up on me and I want to know what was going through your mind that caused you to worry."

She shook her head. "My thoughts weren't important." There was no way she was going to tell him that she'd fallen in love with him. He'd be running as far away from her as he could get, as fast as he could.

"Then tell me what was on your mind." His mouth moved lower, nibbling at her stomach. And then lower.

Jina had gone through this enough over the past few hours. She knew where he was heading and her body wanted his touch there! Badly! She was holding her breath, waiting for him to move lower and when he did, she sighed with relief.

"I'm still waiting, Jina," he said as he blew into her curls that hid her femininity.

She shifted her head back and forth on the bed, refusing to give in to him. She knew that saying those words would cause this affair to end and she wasn't ready! Not yet!

He slipped one finger inside of her, making her gasp out. "Tell me, Jina."

"You can't make me say it, Malik!" she screamed and tried to move away from his tormenting fingers.

Malik only laughed and Jina knew that she was in trouble. "Ah, you think not? Let's just test out your theory, shall we?" and his mouth moved over her heat, his tongue flicking over that nub of nerves and Jina screamed out as his fingers and mouth worked their magic on her body.

Unfortunately, after hours of making love with each other, Malik knew her body too well. Right before she was about to burst into flames with yet another mind-blowing climax, he stopped and she almost screamed out her frustration.

"Tell me what you were thinking, Jina," he said and moved his fingers ever so slightly, blew once again on her overly sensitized flesh.

"You're cheating!" she whimpered and once again tried to move away from his touch.

"Cheating is such a harsh word," he said as he kissed that sensitive spot over her hip. "Let's just say that I'm adept at getting what I want." He kissed her inner thigh and moved his fingers more.

Jina couldn't take it any longer. His fingers and his mouth were too talented and this man knew her body too well. "I love you! I was just thinking about how much I loved you! I love you!" And she arched on the bed, begging him to finish what he'd started.

Malik was more than willing to comply with her silent demands and lowered his mouth once more, his fingers and tongue bringing her over to a screaming climax. Before she had a chance to come down off of that, he'd already sheathed himself in protection and pressed into her tight sheath.

"See? That wasn't so bad," he gritted out between his teeth. "And that only reinforces my decision that we will be married." He moved in and out of her body, moving to give her maximum pleasure. "Very soon!"

Jina wasn't sure what was going on outside of this room. All she knew was that Malik was inside of her and her whole body was splintering apart once again. She'd barely come down off of the previous climax and another was almost upon her. It was like one wave of intense pleasure after another and she could only hang on to Malik's shoulders and trust that he would take care of her through the storm.

And after Malik roared out his own release, he pulled her gently into his arms, cradling her as they both finally fell asleep.

Chapter 5

Jina almost danced down the hallway, too excited as she felt the weight of the ring on her finger. If someone had told her three months ago that she would be dancing down the hallways of a palace, engaged to marry a man like Malik, she would have laughed and dismissed the possibility. It was simply too farfetched!

But here she was and all of her dreams were coming true. It was too fabulous to be real! Malik loved her and she couldn't believe how much she loved him. It was almost like a dream…but not a dream! Her memories of this morning, of the way Malik had woken her up, couldn't be a dream. She had never been capable of dreaming anything so wildly sensuous before meeting this man.

"Food!" she gasped. "I need food!"

She turned to the right versus to the left, heading for the dining room instead of the library where she'd been spending most of her time during the days. She was teaching herself Arabic and loved every nuance of the exotic language. She'd understood a bit of the language before, but now she was really getting into the details, the subtleties of the words. Thankfully, languages had always come easily to her and, although Arabic was significantly different from French or Spanish, the basic rules generally applied across most languages. The trick was to learn the idiomatic phrases that were more a part of culture than they were an aspect of grammar.

As soon as she entered the dining room, she reared back. The smell! Good grief, the smell of coffee was too strong! It was making her stomach churn!

Turning around, she hurried back where she'd come from, not wanting to smell even a hint of coffee.

Wow! Apparently, she hadn't become quite as acclimated to the stronger brew as she'd thought! Never before had she had that kind of a reaction to not just the smell of coffee but the richness of the Arabic blend was much stronger than what she was used to.

Sighing, she realized that her appetite was completely gone. So instead of grabbing a bite to eat, she headed to the library, eager to start her studies again.

After about an hour of studying, Jina felt the headache start to build. No caffeine, she thought with resignation. Maybe a soda would help? But she really wanted a cup of coffee. She wasn't a big fan of sodas.

Standing up and stretching cramped muscles, she looked around and wondered if there was a way to have coffee delivered here instead of walking all the way back to the dining room. She suddenly felt exhausted. She almost laughed at how silly that thought was but, at the same time, she truly was wiped out even though she hadn't done much other than study.

Glancing at her watch, she realized that she'd been awake for less than two hours. Why was she so...?

Jina shook her head. "Of course," she whispered even as she packed up the books and carried them out the door. "No coffee and very little sleep. What did you expect, gal?" she asked herself.

"Sorry," she said when the bodyguard that had been assigned to her looked at her curiously. "I was just going to head towards the dining room for some coffee," she told the man.

His only response was to bow slightly and wait for her to precede him.

Feeling awkward because the man seemed to just be standing around, waiting for her to move, she smiled up at him as an apology. "This is going to take a bit of getting used to,' she told the man. But again, his only response was a slight inclination of his head. "Got it," she said, tapping her stack of books with her thumb. "Dining room. Off we go," she said, almost as if to herself but it really was for the benefit of the guard.

The dining room had already been cleared of breakfast foods but there was a small, silver urn filled with coffee sitting on the side table. Walking over to the pot, she carefully approached, wary of feeling sick again as she had this morning.

Carefully, she poured the coffee into the cup, relieved when her stomach didn't start churning again. Taking a small sip though, made her almost wretch and she set the cup down with a crash. The hot coffee spilled out over the rim and she stepped back, not sure what was happening to her.

"Is everything okay, my lady?" one of the dining room servants asked, appearing suddenly at her side.

Jina was too busy covering her nose with her hand to answer. Lifting up her palm, she nodded her head, trying to convey that she was okay even when she didn't feel okay. She definitely was not okay!

Walking out of the dining room, she hurried down the hallway, forgetting all of the books she'd brought to continue studying. She couldn't help it, her mind was focused only on getting away from that smell.

She hurried down the hallway, pushing through the doorway of the suite she was sharing with Malik and, before she could stop herself, she was falling onto the bed. Jina wasn't even aware of her head hitting the pillow before she fell asleep.

When she woke up again, her hands covered her stomach as the hunger pains hit her hard. Glancing at her watch, she was shocked to find that she'd slept for four hours! She never napped during the day! Even when she worked with clients on assignments that lasted well into the night, she still wasn't able to nap during the day. She'd always just thought it wasn't in her nature.

"You're awake!" Malik snapped, coming over to her and looking angrier than she'd ever thought possible.

Jina cringed back at the look of fury in his eyes. "I'm so sorry! Was I supposed to meet you for lunch?" she asked, trying to sit up but the dizziness was making her more than a little wobbly.

Malik looked down at the woman who had snuck into his heart, furious that she wasn't feeling well but not sure how to help her when she was still trying to hide that trouble from him. "What's wrong? Why have you not eaten and why have you fallen asleep?"

Jina pushed herself up to a sitting position and inched back against the soft pillows. "I can't believe you are asking me that," she commented with a self-conscious laugh.

His only response was to lift his dark eyebrows, silently demanding an explanation.

She shrugged, becoming irritated with his demands. "Are you really going to interrogate me about my sleeping habits when you have kept me up all night, for several nights?" she demanded, standing up and coming towards him.

"Yes," he snapped right back. His eyes noted her pale complexion and the fatigue that was still around her eyes. "You are not well, Jina. You haven't been taking care of yourself."

"I'm fine," she promised, her tone softening when she saw genuine concern in his eyes.

He continued to look at her, then shook his head. "You are not fine. You will stay in bed today."

Her eyes lit up and her body started singing that song that it always crooned when Malik was close by. "Promise?' she asked, laughing softly when she noticed his own body respond.

Malik groaned, rolling his eyes because, just the thought of her desire made him want her even more. "You will stay in bed alone," he told her, even as he pulled her closer to him, gently wrapping his arms around her and kissing the top of her head.

"I don't want to be alone," she replied, lifting her face and breathing in the wonderful scent of the man. Brazenly, she kissed the warm skin of his neck and smiled when she felt the rumble of a groan in his chest.

"No, Jina. You need sleep."

"I just woke up," she told him, letting her tongue dash out to taste him.

She felt his hands tighten on her upper arms and smiled, knowing that she'd won. So when he pushed her away with a shake of his head, she was almost painfully disappointed. "No. You're going to take another nap to get rid of those dark circles under your eyes and, hopefully, that will add more color to your pale skin."

Jina glared up at him, irritated. But then the headache that had been bothering her all morning because she hadn't had any coffee pushed more into her consciousness. Her hand came up, pressing against her temple.

"What's wrong?" he demanded.

Jina shook her head, not wanting to worry him. "Nothing. I just haven't had any coffee yet so I have a caffeine headache."

His hand went to her chin, tilting her head so that he could study her features more carefully. "Why didn't you have any coffee this morning?" he demanded.

Jina saw the worry in his eyes and it hurt her to know that he was worried. She pushed the pain away and smiled up at him, trying to reassure him that she was fine. "I was studying your language," she told him, which was only partly true. "I want to learn to speak it more elegantly before we are married."

His eyebrows popped up with her explanation. "I will endeavor to teach you."

Jina heard the suggestion in his voice and her heart rate accelerated. She looked into his eyes, her whole body coming alive. "Now?" she asked, holding her breath.

Malik only chuckled. "No. Now you will sleep. I will bring dinner here tonight." He laughed again at her frown. "Sleep, my love. We will be married in one month and then we'll have two weeks alone."

Jina sighed with delight. "Promise?" she asked him, pressing her nose against his chest and inhaling his wonderful smell. She couldn't get enough of him, she thought. She'd gone from a prim, prude translator of romance languages to a hussy who couldn't get enough of her fiancé.

"Promise," he assured her. "I have to go," he told her, pulling out of her arms gently. "Get more sleep."

Jina watched him walk out of the room and smiled. She knew that man and he wanted her. He was just trying to be kind with her. Such a sweet, gentle man, she thought.

But she really wasn't tired. Not anymore. The headache was a problem and she went into Malik's bathroom, finding some over the counter painkillers. Hopefully they would kick in and ease the pain quickly.

She found the books she'd been studying earlier, now stacked in the sitting room of Malik's suite and she pulled them over to a table, settling in to study.

"You must leave the palace," a strange voice said from behind her.

Jina lifted her head and looked around. Had she just imagined that voice?

"Get out, and he'll be safe," the voice said again.

A moment later, an envelope slid out from under the chair on which she'd been sitting, stopping right under her foot.

Jina yanked her foot away, startled by the voice and the unexpected movement. "What is this?" she demanded, looking down at the plain, manila envelope but not picking it up. Her stomach was churning at whatever might be inside that package. She knew that she didn't want to see whatever it was. She didn't even want to touch it!

"This is your only warning. If you're not out of the palace by the end of the week…"

Jina waited, swiveling her head around, trying to find out where the voice was coming from. But each time she thought she'd found the source, the voice would come from another direction.

She was trembling now, genuinely terrified and not sure what she should do. "Who are you?" she demanded, trying to sound confident but her voice quivered, giving away her fear. "Why are you doing this?" she asked desperately.

Nothing. No sound. Not even a slight shuffling of feet to indicate someone had scampered away.

When there were no other instructions, she looked down at the envelope. She had to see what was inside, even though she instinctively knew that she wouldn't like it.

Her fingers were shaking as she opened the flap and peered into the package. There were only a few sheets of paper. Pulling them out, she realized that they weren't papers, they were…

Gasping, she dropped the pictures onto the table in front of her and scooted back, reacting as if the pictures were a spider or snake. They weren't alive, but the images burned into her eyes, making her heart stop beating. And then racing forward, speeding and feeling like her heart might just burst out of her chest.

"No!" she cried, her fingers shaking as she looked at the images. "Please no!"

The first one was a picture of Malik in his office and, in the background, she could see the hazy shape of a gun through an ornate screen. She knew that screen! She'd been in Malik's office just yesterday and had commented on it. The workmanship was exceptionally good and she'd run her fingers over the ironwork. She had no idea that an assassin could be hiding behind that screen!

The next picture was of Malik out riding his horse but, as she looked more closely, the image was captured through the scope of a rifle! With Malik in the crosshairs. "No!" she cried out, flipping the picture to the ground.

She was afraid to look at the third picture but she forced herself to review it, afraid not to. Sure enough, it was another of Malik and he was in the dining room. This time, there wasn't a gun anywhere in sight but there was a hand holding a pill. It was just a small pill and if someone hadn't been courteous enough to write "cyanide" on the picture, she wouldn't have known what it was. The implication was that someone was willing to poison Malik.

Looking at the three pictures, she actually had trouble breathing for several moments. And then, it was a race to the bathroom where she threw up. Since there was nothing in her stomach, having skipped breakfast and lunch, there was only the small glass of water and the acid that burned her throat as her stomach continued to churn.

When she finally regained some control of her stomach, she wiped her mouth with a cool washcloth. Unfortunately, that was the end of her control. Her knees gave out on her and she curled up into a ball on the marble floor of the bathroom, so stunned and terrified for Malik's life that she couldn't think properly.

Jina had no idea how long she sat there on the cold, bathroom floor. It might have been minutes or hours, she couldn't determine. All she knew was that Malik was in danger and she had no way to stop someone from hurting him. The pictures obviously were someone's way of telling her that they could kill Malik any way and anytime the culprit chose and her heart ached with the pain of someone hurting him. She couldn't imagine a world where Malik wasn't in it! Goodness, just a few months ago, she hadn't even known the man existed, he hadn't meant anything to her other than as a ruler to a country she'd never visited and never planned to visit. Now he was her life! He meant the world to her and she couldn't let anyone hurt him!

There was a rustling noise out in the sitting room and Jina scrambled off of the floor. She splashed cold water on her face and moved out of the bathroom. She didn't want Malik to see her like this!

Oh no! The pictures! They were still laying on the table in the sitting room!

Stepping into the bedroom, she caught Malik a moment before he stepped into his dressing room. "You aren't sleeping," he cajoled as he pulled his tie loose and disappeared.

Jina watched him for a long moment before her eyes darted to the doorway. Rushing out of the bedroom, she found the pictures and shoved them back into the envelope, hiding everything under the cushion of the sofa.

She'd just finished hiding the horrible pictures when Malik stepped into the doorway, minus his shirt and tie. "What are you doing?" he asked, looking at her curiously.

Jina shook her head, unable to come up with a reasonable explanation since her fear for this man's life was choking her.

Malik walked over to her, looking at her pale features. "You didn't sleep at all this afternoon, did you?" he asked, worried about her. Something was very wrong. She looked like she was about to pass out on him at any moment and her eyes were wide, almost as if...

His body tensed with the fear in her eyes. "You're scared about something. What happened today? Did someone say something to you? Did someone hurt you?"

Jina's mouth opened and closed, not sure how to respond to him. She couldn't lie to him. He always knew when she was lying. But in this case, she had to! His life depended on it.

Taking a deep breath, she forced herself to smile, trying to appear calm and relaxed. "No. No one has said anything to me. I've been here in your suite all day, just studying and lazing around."

His eyes narrowed on her but, after several moments, he accepted her statement. "You didn't leave for any reason?" he asked.

Jina shook her head. "I haven't even peered outside the doorway," she promised. And that definitely wasn't a lie. She'd been curled up in a terrified ball for...well, she had no idea how long.

"I ordered dinner to be served here."

Jina's heart melted with love for this man. He was so kind and generous and trying hard to protect her from something he couldn't understand. She couldn't explain it to him either because she didn't understand it herself. All she knew was that someone was trying to kill this man and she wasn't going to let it happen. Not if she could do something about it.

Malik walked into the bathroom and she heard the shower start up. She bit her lip, trying to figure out what to do. What had the voice said? Get out of the palace or something along those lines. She wasn't exactly sure now. The whole afternoon seemed like a nightmare, one that she couldn't really decipher a beginning or end to.

When she heard him in the shower, she grabbed the pictures and hid them in the closet, worried that he'd suspected something. She was about to hide them in another place when she heard the water shut off.

Pacing back and forth, she bit the end of her thumb, trying to figure out how to save Malik. She'd have to leave. That was an absolute. She'd just leave the palace, go home and pretend she wasn't madly in love with the man. Pretend that her world wasn't destroyed by her departure.

She wished she could say that he wasn't the man of her dreams, but he really was. Oh, he was nothing like the man she'd dreamed she would eventually marry when she was younger. That man was softer, less powerful and so much less of a man than Malik. No, the men she'd come into contact with over the years were so dramatically different from Malik. She knew that she'd never find another like him.

And her whole body ached because, in her heart, she knew she'd never want to find another man like Malik. She didn't want another man, she wanted him. She wanted this man! She'd fought him so hard at first. For those first few days, she'd been determined to not become involved with the man.

Goodness, how easily she'd fallen into his arms! Just one pair of shoes! Those dratted shoes! She should have returned them that first night. She should have dumped them into the trash bin and never looked at them again.

Of course, they were sitting in the closet right now. The closet that had her own clothes intermingled with his. Exactly how she wanted her life to be.

But she wouldn't risk his life. Not even for her own happiness. She loved that man. More than she wanted happiness, she needed Malik to be alive. Even if she couldn't have him, she needed to know that he was here in this world.

And he was a good leader! He genuinely cared about his people! He worked hard to make sure that they had a good life, a fair playing field in which to work and he was honest, believing in the governmental systems but not trusting them. He went to great pains to make sure that the employees who served the people were well taken care of.

So she had to leave. She had to get out of here.

When Malik emerged from the bathroom, he was wearing only a towel around his waist while he rubbed his hair with another one. And he looked amazing! All those muscles covering his tall body. She was mesmerized!

Okay, so she couldn't have him in her life. But she could have him tonight! She could make love to him with all of her heart and all of her soul. She wanted this man. She loved him! And this was her one last night with him.

She'd leave the palace if it meant keeping him safe. But she would add a few memories to savor on those long nights when she'd be alone and lonely. Because no other man could take his place in her heart. Or in her life.

Walking over to him, she placed her hands on his chest, gaining his full attention. Kissing the middle of his chest, she slowly lowered herself until she was on her knees in front of him. When she took him into her mouth, she heard his hiss and a moment later, his hands dove into her hair. From past experience, she knew that his head would be back and his eyes closed so she looked up at him and was so turned on when she realized that he was actually looking down at her, not up at the ceiling or at nothing. His eyes were on her, doing this to him, and that dark look made her increase her efforts. She had done this before, but she was never sure if she was doing it correctly but he seemed to like it. And his enjoyment made her body throb with awareness of her feminine power.

"Jina!" he roared after only a few minutes. His hands lifted her up but he didn't stop with her standing there. He continued until she was in his arms and she wrapped her legs around his waist. He laid her on the bed and quickly stripped her clothes off of her. Then it was her turn to hiss as he impaled her body on his erection.

"Why?" he growled but didn't care at this point in time. He shifted his focus from trying to get an answer from her to making sure that she was feeling just as much pleasure as he was.

When Jina splintered apart in his arms, she felt the tears in her eyes and couldn't hold them back. So instead, she buried her face in the wonderful curve of his neck, hiding her sorrow from this man that she loved so intensely that it was almost a physical need to be with him.

A long time later, he pulled away slightly. "You okay?" he asked gently when he could finally breathe.

Jina laughed. "Yes. I'm fine," she replied, quickly wiping the tears from her eyes so that he wouldn't worry.

But there was nothing this man didn't see. "You were crying!" he noticed and pulled back. "I hurt you! Dammit Jina! I'm so sorry!"

Jina laughed and put her arms around his waist, pulling him back to her. "You didn't hurt me. Just the opposite. You give me so much pleasure, it is all I need." And she kissed the middle of his chest again.

Malik shook his head. "You need food, love," he told her. Pulling back, he used his thumb to wipe away the newest tears. "You haven't eaten all day. Pull on something simple and I'll call the servants. I ordered food to be brought here tonight so we can be alone."

Jina smiled weakly. "That sounds wonderful. Thank you for thinking of it."

She pulled out of his arms slowly, savoring each touch of his rougher skin against hers, loving the way he felt so close to her when they were both completely naked. With regret, she walked into his closet and pulled down a silk robe, wrapping it around her with a sigh. She really was hungry, she supposed. But she'd rather forgo food in order to be in his arms.

But he was already lifting the phone, saying something into the receiver. He glanced in her direction as she came out of the dressing room and, when he noticed she had a robe on, he gave the order to bring in the food. Seconds later, servants appeared through a secondary door and set up a pretty table filled with various foods, then disappeared once again.

Jina chuckled at that kind of service. "You have a charmed life, Malik," she said as she sat down in the chair he pulled out for her.

Taking the seat, Jina opened the folded napkin and placed it on her lap. "What's for dinner?" she asked, always curious. The palace chef was amazing, cooking up elaborate meals for Malik, and her, every night. Malik took off the covers and filled her plate with all of the delicacies. "Eat!" he ordered and sat down across from her, filling his plate even more.

Jina didn't argue. With the smell of food, she realized that she truly was hungry now that her stomach wasn't upset. As they talked about everything and nothing, she devoured more than half the food he'd piled onto her plate, then sat back in her chair, feeling significantly better. The wine was excellent, the food outstanding and she loved listening to him talk about the issues facing him each day.

So when he stood up and pulled her into his arms, she didn't hesitate. She moved with him to the bed, knowing that this was her last few hours with him.

And even after they'd made love again, she still couldn't sleep, too afraid that someone would come to him in the night and hurt him. The pictures showed that, whoever was trying to hurt Malik, could easily get to him. She knew that there were guards outside of the suite, but she still stayed awake, worried that she hadn't left fast enough to save his life. Throughout the night, she beat herself up mentally because she'd been so selfish about wanting one more night with him. It had been wrong! She should have left the palace immediately. So when the morning light filtered through the curtains, and Malik was still alive, she breathed a sigh of relief.

He slipped out of bed, just like he did almost every morning, and she pretended to be asleep. She felt his gentle kiss on her bare shoulder, knew the moment that the shower turned on and off, heard him rustling about in the room, careful not to wake her up. By rights, she should be exhausted. But the possibility of someone hurting this man, simply because she was still with him, kept her awake and terrified for his safety.

When the door clicked shut, she threw off the covers and raced into the bathroom. She showered as quickly as possible, dried off and hurried into the dressing room. Pulling down her suitcase, she loaded her own clothes, leaving all of the fabulous outfits he'd purchased for her. She loved every one of them because she loved the way his eyes lit up when she'd pulled on each outfit for him. But she didn't deserve them now. Nor would she need them. She would go back to her old life, restart her life and figure out some way to get through the days without Malik. Because at least he would be alive. That was all that mattered.

A moment before she closed her suitcase, her hand ran into the horrible photographs and she hesitated. She wanted to tear them up, to shred them and burn them. But she couldn't do it. Not here. She wasn't sure why, she just knew that Malik wasn't meant to feel threatened. Perhaps she was being irrational, but death threats against one's future husband tended to do that to a woman!

As she stood there in the middle of the suite, she looked around, tears streaming down her cheeks, she realized her next challenge was to get out of the palace. If she tried to leave with a suitcase, Malik would be informed. He would stop her, she knew.

Looking down at her suitcase, she realized she'd just have to leave without it. She'd get out of the palace, find a cab and get to the airport. And she'd have to do it all very smoothly so that Malik's guards weren't notified.

With a sigh, she unpacked her suitcase and stuffed it back in the closet. But at the last moment, she took out the Louboutin shoes. She couldn't leave without them! She could leave without everything else, but those shoes…they were the beginning. Well, his glance at her was actually the beginning but these shoes…she might not ever wear them again, but she had to keep them. They were hers. They were a memory of a night when…

She closed her eyes and pushed the memory out of her brain. Stuffing the shoes into her tote bag, she bowed her head as she worked through the details. She didn't really have a plan. Just get out of the palace, go to the airport and catch the first flight out of Sarkit. She knew that it didn't matter where the flight was going, she just had to leave as quickly as possible.

She took several steps forward, then stopped and reached back into the closet. She grabbed the pictures that were stuffed into one of the pockets of the suitcase and jammed them into her big, black leather tote bag.

She checked to make sure she had her passport and wallet, then took a deep breath, and walked out of the suite. She didn't look back, not wanting to think about how wonderful her life had become after Malik's entry to her world.

In the end, it was easier to leave than she'd thought it would be. She told her bodyguards that she was going shopping. They immediately arranged for a car to take her to the market. She stepped out, surrounded by guards but the market was busy and she was able to step out of their sight. From there, it was a simple task to grab a taxi and head to the airport.

She was standing at the ticket counter when it occurred to her that Malik might think she'd been abducted. As the ticket agent clicked away at her computer screen, Jina took her own phone out of her purse and typed in a message to Malik. "*I have to go. I'm not kidnapped. Just going home.*"

She stuffed her phone back into her purse, turning it off so that she wasn't tempted to say anything more, something that might have him coming after her. Like the fact that she felt as if she was dying inside now that she knew she'd never see him again! Or that she needed him more than breathing! Or that he was the most fascinating, gentle, kind and wonderful man she'd ever met in her life!

"There's a flight…" the ticket agent looked up at the woman standing in front of her, her face crumpled into a visage of abject misery. "Ma'am, are you okay?" she asked urgently. "Do I need to call the doctor for you?"

Jina shook her head and tried to pull herself together. "No," she whispered, wiping her tears with a tissue. "I'm fine," she blatantly lied. "The flight?" she prompted. "Where was it going?"

The woman nervously looked down at the screen. "I have a flight to Paris that connects with New York's JFK, but there is a long layover. It leaves in forty-five minutes."

Jina didn't care. "I'll take it," she said and handed the woman her credit card and passport.

Two hours later, Jina was still crying as the plane flew over the earth towards a place she didn't want to be. The only place that she wanted to be was in Malik's arms, in his palace but he was safe now. She could protect him by leaving him.

So who was going to protect her from this horrible feeling inside of her?

"Find her!" Malik roared to his bodyguards.

A man spun around from a computer screen, his eyes nervous as he ventured out a comment. "Your Highness, we have surveillance from the airport," he said.

"Show me!" Malik demanded. The text he'd received from her yesterday just didn't make sense! She'd said she hadn't been kidnapped but why had she left him? After that night…that just wasn't like Jina!

After a few clicks on the man's keyboard, he saw a grainy image of Jina, his beautiful, defiant Jina, standing at the ticket counter. He couldn't see her face from this angle but he could tell that it was her. He'd know her body anywhere! "What is she doing?"

The man cleared his throat. "This was yesterday morning, Your Highness. She bought a ticket to New York City."

Another man spun around in his chair. "She landed at JFK this morning. I've tracked her credit cards and she's staying at a hotel in Manhattan, Your Highness."

Malik stared at the screens. One of them showed her walking down the airport in Sarkit, boarding a plane to Paris. Another showed her stepping of off the jet way in New York City. He wasn't sure if it was due to the quality of the video, but she looked pale. And her eyes…they weren't right.

"Why is she in a hotel?"

The man shook his head. No one knew. "We'll continue to track her, Your Highness."

Turning to his head of security, he glared at the man. "Find her! I want answers! I want to know why she left."

The man nodded his head and turned around, saying something into a phone. Their initial assumption was that she'd been kidnapped but, when no ransom or demands were called in, everyone knew that something strange was going on. Now that the woman had turned up in her old hometown, apparently unharmed, they were more suspicious. This obviously wasn't a kidnapping. So what was it?

Chapter 6

Six Weeks Later…

Jina looked around at her sparsely furnished apartment, fighting back the exhaustion as she dumped her black bag by the door. She would sleep, she told herself. Really, she should eat something, but her mind was too tired to consider fixing food. And she couldn't really face another bowl of cereal or a cup of yogurt which had been her staple meals for the past six weeks since coming back from Sarkit. She'd lost weight and she knew that she looked pretty horrible right now. But she'd gotten a prime job as a translator at the United Nations. So no more clients to manage, no more crazy schedules. Of course, the pay was less, but it came with better health insurance.

Lying down on the bed, she sighed as the mattress slowly took her weight. She'd just rest here for an hour, then get up and have something to eat. Just one hour, she promised herself.

Thirteen hours later, her alarm sounded and Jina jerked awake, looking around, confused and concerned.

Until her stomach started to heave. Then the confusion banished, replaced by panic as she rushed to her tiny bathroom. For several minutes, she prayed that she would survive the nausea. Every morning for the past week, she'd been sick. And in the afternoon, she couldn't get enough food. By the time she arrived back at her tiny apartment, she was exhausted.

There was no way to deny it any longer. She was pregnant.

Closing her eyes, she thought back to her time in Sarkit. They'd been so careful, always using protection. But obviously, one of those times hadn't worked.

Jina pulled herself up and slid the dress from yesterday off, just letting it fall to the floor. It would have to be dry cleaned anyway since she'd slept in it all night.

Turning on the shower, she brushed her teeth while she waited for the water to warm up. Her mind frantically sifted through the realization that she was going to have a baby! Malik's baby! She was going to have his baby!

Wow! Stepping into the shower, she went through the motions but wasn't fully conscious of anything. She was pregnant! A part of Malik was growing inside of her! All of the love she wanted to give to Malik, she could now shower on this tiny human growing inside of her body.

It must have been that last time together. She couldn't remember him donning protection that night, which would mean that she was about six weeks pregnant. What a thrill, she thought! A baby! A precious little boy or girl!

But no, it couldn't have been that last night, she thought, her hands frozen with the shampoo seeping through her fingers. She'd been sick that last morning. The coffee! She hadn't been able to stand the smell of coffee!

Forgetting that there was shampoo in her hands, she covered her stomach with both palms, her mind racing to try and remember their nights together. They were so vivid, but she honestly couldn't remember a time when he'd forgotten protection except for that last night. But maybe one of the condoms had broken? It was possible! When they had made love, she was pretty frantic. And he was a strong, demanding lover, not relenting with his own release until she'd found her own. Could they…?

Only a doctor would be able to confirm how long she had been pregnant.

She shut off the water, not even caring that she hadn't washed her hair. She was too stunned by the thoughts flying through her mind.

Her first instinct was to call Malik and let him know but then she pulled back, realizing that he could never know! She had a series of bookmarks on her computer that she checked every day, looking for news or pictures of Malik. But she couldn't call him, couldn't let him know that he was going to be a father. The realization that he would never know broke her heart all over again, taking away a great deal of the excitement she'd been feeling over the discovery that she was pregnant.

But with that understanding came a newfound sense of life. She had to start eating better. Since she'd left Sarkit, she'd barely been existing. She definitely hadn't been taking care of herself, not eating or sleeping well.

That would all have to change, she told herself as she turned off the water. She hurried to dress herself so that she could eat a healthy breakfast. She wasn't really hungry and her stomach was still churning, but she was determined to put something in her stomach, something healthy so that she could take care of this little baby.

By lunchtime, she had an appointment with an obstetrician and she trembled as she sat in the examining room, wearing a paper gown. She felt ridiculous, but still excited and nervous and thrilled and…a thousand different emotions were zinging through her mind right now.

"Good afternoon," the smiling obstetrician greeted Jina, shaking her hand. "Congratulations!" she smiled, then looked down at Jina's chart. "I understand that you don't remember your last menstrual cycle?"

Jina cringed. "No. I'm sorry. It's been a…" she hesitated, not sure how to explain her life recently. "It's been a crazy few months."

The woman smiled. "I understand. So let's just take a sonogram so we can figure out what's going on and how far along you are. Okay?"

Jina nodded, relieved that she'd have some information since she'd been so completely oblivious to what had been happening inside of her all this time.

The doctor pushed a large monitor into place and Jina leaned back against the hard cushions of the examining table. Warm gel was squeezed out all over her lower tummy which still wasn't showing any evidence of her pregnancy. But as soon as the sonogram machine was turned on, Jina's whole world changed. The tiny image looked larger than life, but it was a life!

"There he is!" the doctor smiled.

Jina's eyes widened. "It's a boy?"

The doctor chuckled. "Sorry about that. I can't tell the gender at this point in your pregnancy. Using the male pronoun is dangerous though."

Jina smiled, but she was still too overawed by the image on the screen. "What is happening?" she asked when the doctor seemed to be taking several measurements.

"It looks like," she wrote down some numbers, "I'm making an educated guess here, but it looks like you are much farther along than you expected."

Jina swallowed past the lump in her throat. "How far along?"

The doctor did several more measurements then smiled. "Well, first of all, the baby looks very healthy. No problems with the development. The heart and spine look good, the arms and legs are forming beautifully and you have plenty of amniotic fluid. So the baby is healthy, but I'm going to put you at about fifteen weeks," she said and wrote down something in Jina's chart. "I'm going to give you a prescription for prenatal vitamins. I want you to start taking them as soon as possible. These are to protect you as well as your baby."

Jina nodded, still stunned by this news. There was still pain and sadness because she couldn't see Malik, and she had to resist the almost overwhelming urge to call him and tell him the news, but it was still wonderful, amazing, shocking, exciting and terrifying!

Jina left the doctor's office with strict instructions to eat more, drink milk several times a day, get the prescription filled, not to mention, get more sleep. And because she was feeling so marvelous all of a sudden, she almost jumped with joy as soon as she was back out on the street.

Everything was going to be okay now, she promised herself. For the first time since seeing those horrible, disturbing pictures, she felt the sunshine on her face, felt as if the world was going to be okay. That she was going to be okay.

More than okay! She was going to have Malik's baby!

Chapter 7

One Year Later…

"Shhhh…" Jina soothed, bouncing gently. "Hush little baby don't you cry…" she sang softly, watching her six-month old daughter's eyes slowly settle against her chubby cheeks, "Momma's gonna sing you a lullaby…"

Bouncing and walking, humming softly, bouncing, walking, humming…more bouncing…standing by Lika's crib…bouncing as she slowly lowered her daughter onto the mattress… "and if that lullaby won't work…" Lika jerked ever so slightly as her back hit the mattress and Jina held her breath, praying that Lika wouldn't wake up again. "Momma's gonna go just a little nuts…." She whispered, still singing along with the tune but changing the words. She was desperate now. It was after eleven o'clock at night and Jina had been up with her teething daughter since about four o'clock that morning.

Jina was exhausted after having worked all day and trying to soothe her daughter all the other hours. She just wanted to sleep! A shower would be nice, but sleep was her top priority at the moment.

She continued to hum as she slowly backed out of the room, dimly lit by the night-light in the corner.

When Jina finally had the door closed, she exhaled slowly as she leaned against the door. Sleep, she almost cried. She was going to sleep until Lika woke up again. She might only have a few hours, but she was going to take whatever she could get.

She stepped into her bedroom and saw the full sized bed, almost crying at how inviting it looked. Inch by inch, she slid herself onto the still unmade bed, pulling her pillow closer. The cool sheets against her skin felt wonderful! She couldn't remember a bed ever feeling so amazingly good. Not even….

Jina sighed and banished those thoughts. He was safe. That's what mattered. Goodness, had this mattress ever felt this soft? She didn't think so.

Just no dreams tonight, she prayed just as her eyes drifted closed.

She was asleep moments later, drifting off to that dreamland.

The doorbell woke her up and her first thought was that someone was going to die! She jerked out of the bed and looked around, wondering if she'd just dreamed the sound. Glancing at the clock, she realized she'd been asleep for about five minutes and her whole body ached at the denial of the essential sleep.

When the doorbell sounded again, she growled, literally growled as she swung her closet door open. She fumbled for only a few moments in her tiny toolbox until she found what she was looking for. With the hammer in her hand, she stormed to the door, determined to stop the possibility of that sound ever happening again.

If she'd had more sleep, Jina might have realized how irrational her next move was. But she was so tired that her bones ached. Right now, Lika was still asleep but that could change at any moment. Her daughter was exhausted too, which was probably the only reason she wasn't screaming her head off at the moment.

Hammer in hand, she swung the front door open and, with one well aimed slam, bashed the doorbell into smithereens! With a satisfied nod, she breathed a sigh of relief that the doorbell couldn't go off again. She then walked back into her apartment, closed the door and was halfway across her living room when she stopped.

Her mind was losing it, she thought.

Malik wasn't outside her door. That was impossible! He was thousands of miles away in Sarkit!

He could not be here!

"Oh no!" she gasped and ran back to the door. Opening it again, she found the man in question still staring at the shattered doorbell, half of it hanging from the wall and the other half in pieced on the ground.

Jina couldn't worry about the doorbell right now. All her worry was for this man. "What are you doing!" she gasped and grabbed him by the lapels, pulling him inside. That wasn't an easy thing to do since the man towered over her. He was a huge man after all, muscles protruding in all the right places and, since she was wearing only socks on her feet, he was about nine inches taller than her.

The only reason she was able to get him into her apartment at all was because of her desperation and his surprise. When he was finally inside, she slammed the door then pulled the curtains closed.

She then turned to look at the man, her eyes wide with fear. "Why are you here?" she demanded. "I'm dreaming this, aren't I?" She pushed her hair out of her eyes and rubbed her face. "This isn't happening. This is all a dream." She looked down at her ratty sweatpants and oversized shirt that should have been thrown away two centuries ago. "No, you are not seeing me dressed like this." She shook her head and plopped down on her sofa. "Nope. This is not a dream. This is a nightmare. Yep," she nodded her head. "It is a nightmare and I'm going to wake up from this and everything will be back to normal." With those words, she sighed and laid her head down on one of the sofa pillows, curling her legs up and started falling back to sleep.

"Jina! What the hell is going on?" Malik demanded as he watched his ex-fiancé drift back to sleep. Had she completely lost her mind?

And what the hell had happened to her? During their entire relationship, she'd never looked this…worn out. There were dark circles under her eyes, her long, dark hair was sticking up at odd angles and her features were pale. He could barely discern her lips because they were the same color as her white skin.

Good grief, had she been stealing her clothes from the garbage cans lately? Those sweatpants were atrocious! Why would she be wearing something…stained and ill-fitting?

If it weren't for Uncle Charles' illness and the man's command to find out why Jina had left him, He still wouldn't have come. Now…well, he only had more questions.

She jerked upright again and looked around, her eyes still not focusing very well. But when they caught him once again, those beautiful, blue eyes widened, obviously forcing her more awake.

"What are you doing here?" she demanded and stood up. "You can't be here! You have to get out of here!"

She glanced around her apartment, trying to figure out what to do. Were they watching even now? They'd sent her pictures throughout the months, proving that they were still watching, still ready to kill Malik if she even thought about going back to him. "Oh no!" she gasped and ran over to him. "Listen Malik, I know this sounds crazy but you have to believe me. Please, just get back on your plane and go back to Sarkit. I'm begging you. That's the only thing that will…" she stopped, realizing how crazy she sounded. "Just leave," she whispered desperately, trying to sound firm but the words came out sounding more like a plea.

Malik had arrived here determined to get answers. Had she just stopped loving him? Had he done something to hurt her? She'd left so abruptly. One night they were tangled in each other's arms and the next day, she was at the airport, buying a ticket with tears in her eyes. When he'd seen more of the video from the airport, he'd been convinced that she'd just left him for no apparent reason and he'd been furious. But now, looking at her in such a bedraggled state, he wasn't so sure that the video had told the whole story.

Something wasn't right.

"What's going on, Jina?" he demanded.

She pushed a hand through her hair, messing it even further. "Oh no! You're guards are outside aren't they? They're watching out for you! They're probably stationed in the parking lot and on the stairways! They'll see!"

Malik was becoming concerned. "What are you talking about? Of course my guards are outside!"

Her eyes widened and she looked up at him. "They have to hide! They have to find cover! I don't know what will happen to them!" She stopped talking and covered her mouth with her hand. "Maybe they won't hurt the guards," she said, obviously talking to herself, pacing back and forth in her small apartment.

She turned back to Malik, more tears forming on her lashes and falling to her pale cheeks. "Please. Couldn't you just…walk away? Pretend that you never found me?" she begged.

Malik was furious that she would even suggest such a thing. Especially when he was now suspecting that she was ill. "Not a chance," he told her firmly.

The wail of a baby startled both of them. His eyes caught her body jerking only moments before she hurried to the back of the apartment.

Malik didn't understand. Surely that wasn't…no, she hadn't….

"Oh please," she whimpered, rubbing her eyes. "Lika, baby, sweet girl. You need to sleep," and Jina walked back into the small bedroom, closing the door once more so that the light wouldn't wake up her daughter even more.

Malik stared at the closed door, his confusion turning to rage as the sound filtered through his brain and he understood that there was a baby in that room, in his ex-lover's arms! The sound didn't stop but he heard her cooing to the baby and his curiosity wouldn't allow him to stand there doing nothing. He had to investigate. Because the possibility that Jina, his beautiful Jina, had a child was inconceivable! That would mean that another man...

Impossible!

But as he stood in the doorway, he watched with morbid fascination as the woman who had haunted his dreams, his former fiancée, bent over a crib and lifted a tiny, crying baby into her arms. Her gentle hands cradled the soft, fuzzy head even as she started bouncing the baby, trying to soothe the infant's temper.

"You woke her up!" Jina snapped. The baby started crying louder and Jina bounced harder.

"It's going to be okay, my love," she soothed. Jina slipped her finger into the baby's mouth but Malik had no idea why. Somehow that seemed to soothe the child even as Jina reached for something on the baby's dressing table with the hand that was holding the infant. Apparently she'd grown a couple of limbs in the time it took her to disappear because there was no way two arms could be accomplishing everything. "Here you go, love. This will help. Just let me..." she handed the tube to Malik. "Can you open this for me?" she asked.

Malik looked down at the item she handed to him and realized that it was teething gel. That started to make sense and he opened the top. What he knew about babies could fill a thimble but he had heard that babies teethed and they cried a lot. Among other actions that they did a lot, he thought with revulsion.

"You have a baby," he growled, trying to come to terms with the fact that his Jina was a mother now. He was furiously jealous, he could barely stand still.

Jina ignored him, focusing all of her attention on the tiny girl in her arms. She squeezed a bit of the teething gel out onto her finger, then rubbed the infant's gums. Instantly, the baby stopped crying but Jina still lifted the child into her arms again. "Yes, I have a baby," she told him finally.

"How old is this child?" he demanded. He wanted to know how soon after she'd left him that she'd jumped into another man's bed.

"She is six month's old," Jina replied and sat down in the rocking chair, holding her daughter close.

Malik stood in the center of the room, his mind mentally doing the math. If this child was six months old, that would mean that Jina…she'd been three months pregnant when she'd left him!

That would mean that…he stared at the baby in Jina's arms, his mind frantically trying to come to terms with what that meant.

"Jina…?" He looked at the little girl with the dark head of fluff. Not hair yet, but it would soon be hair. It was just soft fuzz at this point. "Is that…?"

Jina patted the baby's back as she rocked back and forth, trying to get the baby back to sleep. "Is this your daughter?"

Malik could barely nod his head.

"Yes. This is Lika," she finally admitted. "This is your daughter."

Jina watched as the emotions flitted across Malik's handsome face. She was startled by the final one. Awe was a powerful emotion, she realized and Malik moved closer, his hand reaching out to touch her baby girl. His baby girl. She watched with fascination as his strong fingers touched his daughter for the first time. He was so tentative, almost nervous.

"I have a child?" he asked, still not believing it.

She nodded her head, unaware of the tears that slipped down her cheeks. The past year had been so hard and so wonderful. She'd had to leave this man, leave him so that he was protected. But the realization that she was pregnant with his child had helped her through the devastation of leaving him. She'd always thought that God had been cruel to have ripped the man she loved out of her arms but then she'd discovered that she was pregnant with his child and she realized that God had given her a piece of Malik to cherish forever.

But then she realized what was going to happen and fear welled up inside of her. She looked down at her daughter, falling asleep once again, her dark, brown eyes, so similar to her father's, were closed now.

"You have to leave," she urged as panic threatened to choke her. "You have to leave and pretend that you don't know anything about Lika. Please, Malik. Get out and never come back!"

Malik couldn't believe what he was hearing! Leave his daughter? Leave her now that he'd just discovered that he was a father?

"That is out of the question," he told her without hesitation. He lifted his cell phone out of his pocket and dialed a number. "Come quickly," he said in Arabic, obviously to his guards.

Moments later, her apartment door burst open and five very large, heavily armed men stormed into her apartment, weapons drawn and looking around for the danger to their ruler.

Malik walked out, lifting his hands to calm them. "I have a daughter," he told them, shocking each and every one of them. "We need to get both of them to a secure environment."

The lead guard lifted his radio and spoke rapid commands. From that moment on, Jina knew that her night was gone. She'd get no rest tonight and she almost cried at that realization. "Please," she begged. "Don't do this. I'm so tired and Lika is tired. She's teething and we haven't slept very well for the past few nights." Jina tried very hard to pull herself together, but she was just so tired! And Malik was so handsome, she just wanted to throw herself into his arms and sob out her fear and sadness over the loss of what could have been between them. What could never be!

Malik looked down at the woman holding his child and he hardened his heart. "You and the baby will be taken care of," he told her.

She shook her head. "No! You don't understand! They told me..." she bit her lip, not wanting to scare him.

Malik caught her slip and his eyes narrowed on her pale features. "What were you going to say, Jina? Has someone threatened you?" he demanded. That would make some of her earlier comments make sense.

Jina's lips compressed. Once she'd retreated to New York, a phone call had relayed her additional threats. She'd been told not to say anything, that it would only make it worse. Just get out of Sarkit, the raspy voice had commanded. If she stayed away without giving anything away, no one would get hurt. If she told anyone, there would be more casualties.

Malik looked down at her and knew that there was a great deal more to the story. But she wasn't going to say anything and he recognized the terror in her eyes. Something had happened. And damn it, he should have come after her sooner! This was his fault, he berated himself.

"Let's go," he told her.

She shook her head. "Please Malik. Just leave," she whispered desperately.

Malik moved over to her, taking her upper arms in his hands and that's when he realized how badly she was trembling. "We're leaving, Jina. I have to get you and the baby to a secure area. My guards can't protect us here and I'm not leaving without you and the baby." His eyes looked down into her blue ones, trying to convey how serious he was about this. "If there is danger, then staying here will only increase the odds that someone can get to me or you. Or the baby," he added, looking again at the infant now sleeping in Jina's arms. "You know me. You know that I won't leave now. So…"

"Fine!" she snapped. "Let's go! But you have to promise me that, once you've heard everything, you'll leave and forget us."

He almost rolled his eyes. "I am eager to hear everything," he promised. There was no way he was going to pretend that he didn't know that he had a child though. And if what he suspected was true, he would be married to this woman by the end of the day. Glancing at his watch, he corrected himself. He would be married to her by the end of tomorrow since there was only a half hour left in the current day.

She followed Malik out of the apartment but stopped, grabbing her keys. "I need…"

"You don't need your car, Jina," he told her firmly.

"I need the car seat in my car. Lika needs to be safe," she told him, not budging on this issue.

Malik looked at her for a moment, then nodded his head to one of his guards.

"The car seat is by the door," she told him. And I need the bag there too. Both bags," she told the guard who lifted the first one. "Oh, and I need my briefcase," she announced and started back to her room. She hadn't finished the work she'd brought home because Lika had been crying all night. The pain in her gums had been too much for the little lady to handle. Jina had planned on getting up early tomorrow morning to get the work done.

"You're no longer working," Malik announced with an air of absolute authority.

Jina heard those words and shook her head. "Yes I am," she told him and slipped the briefcase stuffed with work on her shoulder. "I have to pay the rent."

Malik didn't respond. There was no way his woman was going to work any longer. "Are you still working at the United Nations?" he asked.

"Yes. And they have an important meeting tomorrow. I'm on the schedule to translate."

Malik didn't say a word, but he gave his guard a look. The other man nodded his head, knowing that phone calls would have to be made. By morning, Jina would no longer be eligible to work at the United Nations. One couldn't be married to a ruler and still work in the United Nations. He wasn't sure it was a written rule, but he'd wager a great deal of money that it was a pretty strict guideline.

It took several minutes to get the car seat tightened properly in the limousine. But once it was in, Jina transferred Lika to the carrier and gently strapped her in without waking her up. The fact that she slept through all of this only proved how exhausted her tiny daughter really was.

Fifteen minutes later, the limousine was pulling into the underground parking lot of the Ritz Carlton and the guards were fanning out, looking for dangers. Jina carried her still-sleeping daughter into the hotel, right up to the penthouse suite. "Goodness," she sighed, remembering the luxury that always surrounded Malik.

"Put her in one of the rooms and then let's talk."

Jina shook her head. "Could we please talk later?" she asked, setting Lika down and rocking her gently.

Malik nodded his head. "You're right. We have other priorities." He turned to his guard and raised an eyebrow.

"Five minutes," the guard stated.

Malik nodded. "Fine. Do you want to change clothes?" he asked Jina.

Jina shook her head. "No. I'm fine. I just need to sleep."

"Here," he said and handed her a glass filled with a dark liquid.

Jina glanced at the glass briefly but shook her head. "I can't."

He stared at the liquid. "You used to love brandy," he told her accusingly.

Jina stood up and looked at Malik. "I can't drink alcohol. Not while I'm..." she couldn't finish that sentence. Her cheeks turned pink and her mind blanked out.

Malik didn't understand. "Why not?" he demanded. "You were never a heavy drinker before. What's changed?"

Jina shifted on her feet. "I just…can't," she told him and turned back to Lika, adjusting the blanket unnecessarily over her daughter. She had trouble looking at Malik when discussing something so intimate.

Malik stared at the top of her head, wondering what was going on. He rubbed the back of his neck and tried to come to terms with everything he'd learned tonight, hoping something would make sense.

"Jina…" he started to say only to be shushed by her.

"She's asleep and she's going to stay that way. She's so tired," and Jina touched her daughter's head softly.

"You are exhausted as well. And you're not making sense, Jina. Or at least, no sense that you're willing to explain to me."

The door opened behind her and a new man walked in.

Jina stared at the man, confused.

"Who is he?" she demanded, worried about any strangers.

There was quite a bit of shuffling as the guards consulted with Malik who had a short conversation with the stranger. In the end, no one really explained anything, but Jina was too tired to understand, so she didn't care. As long as Lika slept, she was happy. Well, she'd be happier if she could also sleep, but…

Malik took her hands in his and turned her to the other man. Guards stood on either side of them and the man started speaking.

"Do you take this woman to be your lawfully wedded wife?" he asked Malik.

"I do," he said quickly. Jina's mouth fell open with those words.

Turning to Jina, the stranger said, "Do you take this man to be your lawfully wedded husband?"

Jina looked at the man, stunned. He was marrying them? Impossible! "No!" she snapped and started to pull back.

Malik turned her to face him. "Jina, we are to be married. And it has to be quickly and in secret. This man is here to marry us in the quickest way possible. And then we're going to get to the bottom of all the issues surrounding your abrupt departure a year ago. So just say the correct words and we can move on."

Jina shook her head but Malik squeezed her hands, telling her that she wasn't getting out of this. "I do," she finally said but her eyes were blazing her fury at him. A fury that was hiding her fears.

The man continued to mutter some words but Jina didn't hear anything after that. The man bowed, slipped a piece of paper for both of them to sign and moments later, he walked out. Jina stood there, stunned.

She looked around and found Malik conferring softly with his guards. They all looked extremely serious as they looked up to him and she shivered, thinking she'd just sentenced this man to death.

"Please, Malik. Tell me that we weren't just married!"

Malik turned and looked over at her, surprised to find her almost in tears again.

He walked over to her and took her hands. "Will you please explain?" he asked softly.

She knew that she was gripping his hands too tightly but her fear was overwhelming her. "They're going to kill you! He told me that!"

Malik didn't even blink an eye. "Who is going to kill me?"

"I don't know!" she sobbed. "I didn't get to see his face. I only know what he said."

The guards moved closer, obviously furious that someone had breached their security. "Where did it happen? What day?" He held up a hand to stop her. "Wait, it was the day before you left me, wasn't it?" he guessed.

Jina nodded her head, clasping her hands behind her back.

"And you left me without telling me what was going on?" It was a question, but she didn't really think she needed to answer it.

"I wasn't…"

"Stop, Jina," he told her, his voice more gentle now. "I understand."

She shook her head. "No. You don't understand anything. But I'm too tired right now to help you understand." She glanced at her watch and sighed. "I have about three hours before I have to be up and get ready for work. I'm going to find a place to fall asleep and then I'll get out of your life again tomorrow."

She should probably head back to her apartment tonight but everything was just too confusing. She didn't want to deal with this right now. She just needed a bed and…nope, she didn't even need a pillow. A bed would suffice. Even flat surface would work.

She opened the first door she came to and found an empty bed. Carrying Lika into the room, she set her on the floor, then curled up next to her daughter, worried that Lika would wake up in the middle of the night and not know where she was. She pulled the covers and the pillows down to the floor, curled up and was instantly asleep.

Chapter 8

Malik finished discussing security with his guards then made several phone calls to his chief of staff, giving him instructions. By the time he hung up the phone, dawn was almost breaking over the horizon and he was exhausted, but Malik knew that he wouldn't be able to sleep.

He opened the door to the room where he knew his family was sleeping and was shocked to find Jina on the floor curled up around the baby carrier. There was no need for her to sleep there. He moved his still-sleeping daughter out of the way, then lifted Jina up and placed her onto the bed. Covering her up, he looked at her for several long moments. She was still beautiful despite the fatigue that had caused her complexion to turn into the color of bland oatmeal instead of the peaches and cream he remembered from the last time they'd been together.

Damn, he thought. She'd been trying to protect him all this time! What a little lioness, he thought. All of the anger and resentment he'd been feeling since the day she'd left him dissolved with this new information. She shouldn't have left him, he thought. She should have come to him and explained what she'd heard.

It was probably a prank, he thought. No one who entered the palace would dare to threaten him. It was treason and punishable by death. But his beautiful Jina wouldn't know how thoroughly the palace staff was investigated before they were allowed to enter the palace. Only Jina had gotten close to him before she'd been thoroughly investigated by his guards. Only she'd broken through to his heart.

And now she was back and he wasn't going to ever let her go. Never again.

The tiny human being squawked as if she were about to wake up. He glanced over at Jina, then down at the baby. His daughter!

Just thinking those words sent a thrill through his body. He had a daughter!

Malik lifted the carrier and brought the little baby into the living room. Setting the carrier on the table, he simply stared at the tiny baby, amazement running through him. He inventoried all of her features, trying to see himself in her face. But with her eyes closed, he wasn't sure. Her skin was darker than Jina's but…

And then those tiny eyes opened up and he was staring at his own dark eyes. Something in his gut twisted and he was spellbound.

His daughter wasn't one to wait around though. When she wasn't immediately lifted up, she opened her tiny mouth and let out a scream louder than he thought possible coming from a human that size.

His guards came running into the room, weapons drawn as they looked around for the threat. When their eyes all focused on the tiny human being, they quickly put their weapons away.

His head of security, Aaron, came closer at the sound. Malik and Aaron looked down at the baby then to each other. "What should I do?" Malik asked, which was an odd question since Malik always knew what to do. But those situations had to do with oil prices, stock prices, property values and politics. The concept of how to care for a baby was beyond both of their experience.

"Wake up your wife," Aaron stated firmly, as if that were the only option.

The baby screamed harder, getting her arms and legs into the effort as they wiggled in the air. Malik could just wake up Jina, but he didn't want to do that. She was exhausted and had been caring for their child for the past six months. Longer if he counted her pregnancy.

"Maybe pick her up?" Aaron suggested.

Malik looked back down at the baby. "Probably the right thing to do," he replied. But still he stared, wary of picking up such a tiny human being. He was a large man with large hands. He was worried that he might hurt the infant. But in the end, the little girl's face was turning red with her rage at not being picked up, so he relented, determined not to hurt his daughter with his big hands.

It took him several minutes to figure out how to open straps of the baby carrier off of her tiny shoulders but when the clasp was finally released, the little girl tried to lift her body out. She was too small yet to do that so Malik lifted her into his arms.

The crying instantly stopped as father and daughter stared at each other for the first time. The little girl had the most atrocious frown on her face as she tried to figure out if the person holding her was good or bad. She still hadn't made up her mind yet, but looking around, she realized that her mother wasn't in sight.

Her lower lip quivered slightly and Aaron rushed over to the bag. "Maybe she needs food?" he suggested.

There were several bottles of baby food in the bag along with diapers and a change of clothes. "Or a diaper change?"

Malik felt the baby's bottom and, sure enough, it felt heavy. "Okay, so change her," he said, starting to hand the girl over to the guard.

The girl looked over at the other man and opened her mouth to cry again. "No no!" Malik soothed, bringing her back to him. Instantly, his daughter went back to simply frowning, glaring at the other man as if he were the enemy.

Malik looked over at Aaron who was enormously relieved to not have diaper duty. "Okay, so now what?" he asked.

Another guard walked in and saw what was going on. "There's probably a changing thing in the bag," he explained.

Malik looked at the other guard curiously. "What's a changing thing?" he asked.

The man's hands dove into the bag and came up with a plastic covered pad. "My wife lays our son down on this when she changes his diaper."

Malik took the pad and laid it on the coffee table. "Now what?" he asked.

The other man shrugged his massive shoulders. "No clue. I get out of there fast."

Malik sighed. "You're not helping," he said to the other man.

Aaron smothered his amusement. The three men examined the baby's clothes. "I think those snaps at the bottom come open."

Malik laid the little girl down on the table and tried to unsnap the bottom of her cotton outfit. But her tiny legs kept getting in the way. "Stay still!" he commanded to his daughter.

The little girl wiggled even more, trying to catch his hands. Finally, Malik took the cotton outfit and just pulled. The bottom miraculously came apart to reveal a very wet diaper. Three men pulled back, horrified at the idea of changing the diaper.

"Now what?" Malik asked, keeping a hand on his wiggling daughter's tummy so she didn't fall off of the coffee table.

Aaron handed Malik the clean diaper and the three men stared at it. "How does it open up?"

Aaron took it back, fiddling with it but he eventually figured it out and handed it back to Malik. "Okay, so how do I get the other one off?"

Once more, the men stared at the tiny human. Finally, Aaron handed Malik a lethal looking knife. Malik looked up at the man with an Are-You-Kidding look. The man sheepishly put the knife away. "Scissors then," he said and instantly moved away to search in the kitchen for a pair of scissors. He came back moments later with a pair and Malik carefully cut the wet diaper away from his daughter and pushed it away from all of them.

She was obviously loving this because she smiled and wiggled her arms and legs faster, looking at the three men curiously. It still took Malik several tries to get the dry diaper underneath her tiny bottom and between her legs. But then the next problem surfaced. "Okay, now how to I keep it closed?" he asked, looking back up at the two guards that had grown to four. All of whom shrugged their shoulders.

"Tape!" one of them snapped and he raced away in search of tape.

A few minutes later, he came back with an enormous roll of silver duct tape. "Really?" Malik asked, looking suspiciously at the roll of industrial strength tape in his hands.

Aaron shrugged as well. "Do you have a better idea?"

Malik tilted his head in acknowledgement. "Good point." And he pulled a long strip of duct tape, ripping it off with his teeth. With one hand, he held his daughter and with the other, he laid the tape over the diaper, sealing it shut. "That worked," he said with a great deal of satisfaction. "Now how do I close this thing?" he asked, referring to the clothing.

All of a sudden, he was alone with just Aaron, the two men looking around and both wondering where the other guards had vanished. "Cowards," Aaron grunted.

Malik bent lower, looking at the material. "I think I just close the snaps again."

It took fifteen minutes, but Malik eventually got both of his daughter's legs back in the material and the snaps closed up. When he was done, he lifted the tiny girl up into the air, a feeling of success coming over him. "There!" he said, proud that he'd changed his first diaper. He'd taken care of his daughter!

Aaron stood behind his ruler and grunted in appreciation. "Now you have to feed her," he said and stepped back. "I'll go out and get supplies," he explained, backing away quickly so that his boss wouldn't ask any more questions. That was the extent of his knowledge of babies and he was sticking to it!

Malik glared at the man's retreating back but he was determined to figure this out.

Jina woke up and stretched, feeling better than she had in a long time. She snuggled down into the soft, warm bed and closed her eyes, enjoying the moment of pleasure.

But then she realized what was wrong! Lika! She was missing!

Jumping out of the bed, she almost slipped on the wood floor in her cotton socks. Where was her daughter? She'd fallen asleep on the floor and Lika had been right next to her! She was sure of it! And then the memories from the night before flooded back to her and she gasped. "Malik!"

She almost screamed his name, wanting to get to him and tell him that someone had taken Lika! She raced out of the room, searching frantically for Malik. She'd warned him that this would happen! She'd told him to just leave! To go back to his country and everyone would be safe!

She came to a skidding halt when she walked into the enormous living room and found Malik on the floor, her tiny daughter sitting on a blanket surrounded by new toys. And Lika was laughing! Her little baby girl was laughing!

She just stared for a long time, watching Malik play with their daughter. Oh goodness, she thought she'd never see this! The threat to Malik's life had convinced her that Lika would never know her father but here he was! And she seemed to have accepted him completely.

Jina watched as Lika stuffed one of the plastic rings into her mouth. Or tried to. The ring was too big but she rubbed her gums on the toy, making them feel a little better.

"She's okay," Jina whispered, relief surging through her.

Her words caused both father and daughter to turn and look at her. Malik's sexy eyes went up and down her figure and she looked down, realizing that she was still wearing those hideous sweats and tee-shirt along with the boring white sox.

"Good morning," she said self-consciously, pushing her hair back behind her ear and wishing she'd remembered to bring a change of clothes with her last night.

Malik lifted Lika up into his arms and stood up, coming over to her. "Good afternoon," he corrected.

Jina glanced out the window, surprised to see that the sun was higher in the sky than she'd anticipated. "What time is it?" she asked.

"Two o'clock," he replied and adjusted Lika on his hip.

Jina gasped, her hands going to her forehead. "Oh no! I didn't call in sick to work! I didn't tell them that I wouldn't be in today! I'm going to be fired! It was an important day!"

Malik looked at her shirt. "Are you okay?" he asked, noticing the wet spots appearing on her shirt.

Jina glanced down and wished that the earth would just swallow her up. "Oh no!" she sobbed, covering her breasts with her arms. "I haven't fed Lika yet," and she reached for her daughter. "Please," she said and blinked back the tears. "I need to feed her."

Malik released his daughter into Jina's arms and watched with fascination as she walked back out of the room. "Where are you going?"

"I need to feed Lika," was all she said.

Jina found a chair in the corner of the room she'd slept in and pulled her daughter closer. Lika knew instantly what was going on and eagerly found her lunch. Jina closed her eyes, feeling the release of her milk as her daughter nursed. And the whole time, Jina tried to figure out what was going on.

Okay, it is afternoon, she told herself. And she'd missed work. She could fix this, she thought. She could just call in to her supervisor and tell them what was going on. But this had been an important day. She wasn't sure her supervisor would accept any excuse.

Lika nursed from one breast and then Jina shifted her over to the other. Thankfully, Lika was hungry and it took less than a half hour before her belly was full and Jina's breasts felt much better.

"I didn't know you were breast-feeding," Malik said from the doorway.

Jina jerked and twisted around, staring at him in horror. "How long have you been standing there?" she asked.

Malik pushed away from the doorframe, walking towards her. "Long enough. It was beautiful," he told her. "You're a very good mother."

She pulled her tee-shirt down, painfully self-conscious of the ugly nursing bra she had to wear. "Thank you," was all she could say in reply. Jina felt too self-conscious sitting here in the bedroom with Malik looking down at her. She stood up and walked out of the bedroom, needing space and a place that didn't have a bed.

Back out in the elegant living room, she blinked at the sight in front of her. Jina wasn't sure what was going on so she rubbed her forehead, trying to understand. Gone was the beautifully decorated room and in its place, a nursery had exploded with toys and every conceivable baby contraption ever invented. She looked around, confused. "Where did all of this come from?"

Malik glanced at the room, but his eyes were drawn right back to his daughter and the woman who had mysteriously walked out of his life a year ago. "I had one of my guards go out and pick up a few items."

Jina looked at the floor that was now covered with toys, a large, soft blanket, a baby swing, high chair, stroller…as if she could take Lika out now!

The danger was higher now! There would be no casual strolls through the park today or any day in the near or distant future!

"We have to go," she said, unable to look at Malik. She cuddled Lika closer, smelling her daughter's sweet, baby scent to reassure herself that Lika was still okay.

Malik crossed his arms over his chest. "You're not leaving, Jina. I don't understand why you left but we're going to solve this. You were too tired last night to make any sense, but do you think you could sit down and explain things now?"

Jina looked around at the beautiful penthouse, the ambiance destroyed by the baby paraphernalia. "No. It isn't safe. Not for you or for Lika." She sent him a pleading look. "Please, Malik. Just go back to Sarkit and pretend that you don't know about Lika."

He almost laughed at her plea. "Would you be able to leave her?" He moved closer, noticed the rapid pulse at the base of her slender neck. "Would you leave Lika with me and promise never to see her again? Never ask about her? Never know what she's doing or see her smiles?"

"No," Jina replied furiously.

Malik nodded. "Good. Then don't ask me to do that. I know about her. I've spent the last several hours with her. I can't leave my child."

Jina's eyes teared up because the danger was so very strong. "You have to."

"I won't. You're going to talk to my head of security. I'm going to hire a nanny and we're going to get to the bottom of this."

Jina pulled Lika closer. "NO! No nanny! You don't know how deep this goes."

Malik sighed and rubbed a hand over his neck. "Be realistic, Jina. You can't take care of Lika all the time. Even now, your arm is getting tired of holding her."

Jina looked down at Lika who was happily gnawing on the colored, plastic donut. "I'm fine," she argued.

Malik rubbed the back of his neck, knowing that she was probably still too tired right now. "How about this. Why don't you go take a shower, which might help you feel better? I'll have some coffee ready for you…"

"No coffee," she told him.

His eyes narrowed. "You love coffee," he argued.

She shook her head, feeling her cheeks turn red once again. "Malik, please…just…no coffee."

And in that instant, his narrowed eyes dropped to her breasts, the heat zinging throughout her whole body with that gaze. "Ah," was all he said for a long moment - a moment when his eyes didn't leave her breasts and she felt her nipples harden in reaction. She shifted Lika so that she was in front of her instead of on her hip and Malik chuckled, a soft, sexy sound that made her body ache. She remembered that laugh! Oh goodness, he'd made that sound when they were in bed together and he did something she liked!

She took a deep breath, trying to clear her mind. "A shower would be wonderful though."

"Do you trust me to watch Lika while you shower?" He moved closer. "Or I could watch you."

Jina gasped at that offer. And boy, she wished she could take him up on it! She missed him so much! All she wanted was to throw herself into his arms and feel his strength and power. She remembered so many nights in his arms and he'd never left her wanting.

With trembling arms, she offered their daughter to him.

Malik reached out and took hold of Lika and, thankfully, he had a good grip on her because the back of his hand slid against her breast. Her eyes slashed up to his as her body reacted. Had he done that on purpose? Looking at his features, she was pretty sure that the innocent expression on his face was feigned. Malik was never innocent!

"I'm going to shower," she told him and crossed her arms over her chest, trying once again to hide her reaction. "Alone," she asserted firmly, just in case he got any naughty ideas. Which he always did.

She heard him chuckle as she walked away which only proved her point about his innocence. Non-existent!

She went back to the bathroom attached to the room she'd slept in, vaguely noticing that the bed was already remade even though she hadn't seen any of the staff. But she was too eager for a shower to think about where the staff might be hiding. She quickly stripped off her clothes and stepped into the warm shower, reveling in how wonderful it felt to be clean once again. And well rested! Oh goodness, the world seemed like a completely different place after a good night's sleep!

She used the scented shower gel all over her body, hoping that it would help her skin soften after months of neglect. She lathered her hair twice with the hotel's shampoo. Not because her hair was especially dirty, but more because the shampoo just smelled so amazing and the lather was soft. After conditioning her hair and rinsing once more in the warm spray, she turned off the water and dried her body with the soft, fluffy towels. When she stepped out of the shower, she saw her clothes on the floor and sighed. Goodness, she really didn't want to put those back on!

But she picked them up off the floor and stepped out into the bedroom, prepared to just wear these clothes until she could get back home and grab something different. She wondered if she could fit back into her skinny jeans. Had she lost enough of the pregnancy weight? She hadn't had the courage to even try them on. Nor did she look in the mirror without clothes on. She was just too afraid of what she might see. Her body had changed so much during pregnancy. Would she look the same? Had her figure come back? The look in Malik's eyes suggested that it was possible, but what did he know?

As soon as she stepped into the bedroom, she stopped in her tracks. Laying on the bed was a pair of beautiful black slacks and a burgundy cashmere sweater. She reached out and touched the sweater, feeling the incredible softness. It was also a cardigan, so she could nurse more easily. Oh my, she thought with relish as she investigated the pile of luxurious clothing. There was even sexy underwear! She couldn't wear the bra, her current, hated maternity bra a necessity for nursing, but goodness, she would love to feel the lace panties against her skin.

Could she do it? Could she wear these clothes, even knowing that she couldn't stay with Malik? She looked down at the ancient, stretched out tee-shirt and the stained sweat pants. Yes. She could definitely wear these clothes! Now that she had an alternative, there was no way she was going to let Malik see her in those horrible clothes again. A woman had pride, she thought!

Tossing the old ones into the garbage can, she eagerly slipped the slacks on, praying that they would fit her. When she slid the zipper up and buttoned the waist, she felt a hundred percent better! And the burgundy sweater slid over her skin like a soft caress. Oh my, she thought and ran her hands over the material one more time.

There were even shoes, a cute pair of two-inch heels that gave her a bit more confidence.

She found a hair dryer and styled her hair, realizing that she desperately needed a trim. She hadn't been to a hairdresser in…well, since before she'd met Malik! Goodness, her hair was a mess. She pulled it into a bun but didn't have the pins to hold it there. It would just have to fall around her shoulders like a tangled mess, she realized.

She had makeup, but it was in her purse which was out in the living room. At least, she hoped it was in the living room. Last night was a bit of a blur and she wasn't sure what was going on right now.

So, fresh faced and freshly cleaned, she stepped back out into the living room feeling much more human.

"What have you done with my daughter!" she cried out when she saw her daughter hanging from Malik's hands. "Don't you dare get close to her baby skin with those scissors!" she yelled just as Malik's guard was about to…well, she had no idea what he was about to do.

She took in the guard, looking stunned with the scissors frozen halfway in the air, Malik holding Lika up with both hands, and Lika dangling in the air, her tiny legs wiggling and a smile on her face as if all of this was simply a happy moment in her life.

"She needs a new diaper. We're just going to get the diaper off of her," Malik explained, then nodded to Aaron again to go ahead with the scissors.

"Stop!" she called out again. Once more, everyone froze. Well, everyone except Lika who had no idea what a dangerous situation she was in at the moment. "Explain why you need scissors to get a diaper off. And what in the world is that pink stuff?"

Malik and Aaron both looked at Lika's chubby tummy, then back to her. "That's duct tape."

She shook her head and closed her eyes. "Duct tape is silver. That's pink! Duct tape is not pink!" She then opened her eyes and glared at the two men, not daring to look at her daughter again.

Aaron grimaced. "Well, ma'am, we ran out of the other kind. When we called down for more, the hotel didn't have the silver kind but one of the maids had this so they sent that up for us."

Jina's mouth fell open and she tried to work through what they were telling her. But it just didn't make any sense. "Let me see if I understand this correctly." She paused, her hand moving to her forehead as she sorted through everything they'd just told her. "Lika needed a new diaper and, instead of just using the convenient tabs on the side of the diaper, you've duct taped the diaper together. And you've used so much duct tape that..." she paused because the hilarity of the situation was just too much for her to go on with a straight face, "that you had to request more from the hotel staff and they sent up the craft type of duct tape." She looked at her daughter who was still grinning and wiggling. "And you have to cut the diapers off with scissors."

Malik pulled Lika closer. "It was scissors or a knife," he explained, then muttered a curse when he saw Jina's eyes widen in horror. "I probably shouldn't have mentioned that part."

Aaron knew when to retreat and he did so quickly, leaving the scissors on the table. Malik saw the man depart and shook his head. "Now who is the coward?" he muttered under his breath.

Facing Jina, he held out his hand. "I'd at least like you to acknowledge that I figured out how to change her diaper. I understood how nervous you were about getting in a nanny so the only alternative was to do it myself. And you got more sleep, right?"

She wasn't sure if she should laugh or be angry with him. Instead, she walked over to him and took her daughter out of his arms. "Duct tape? Really?" She then walked over to the table where the changing mat was laying along with bags of diapers that were lined up against the wall. She had no idea how long he was planning to stay here in this penthouse suite but he was fully prepared with diapers for the next millennium.

She tore the pink duct tape away...or at least she tried to tear it away. The diaper tore but it didn't come apart. The stupid diaper had so many layers, so much stuffing! The stupid thing didn't look like it had this much inside of it!

"Good grief!" she groaned. After several more minutes of trying to get the obnoxious diaper off, she glared at him as she grabbed the scissors, ignoring his chuckle as she cut the stupid thing off.

She grabbed another diaper and made short work of putting the dry diaper on. "Tabs!" she showed him, lifting the small tabs on each side of the diaper. When the diaper was secure, she efficiently stuffed Lika's legs back into the onesie and lifted her up into her arms. "Tabs, Malik," and smacked the scissors against his chest before walking away to sit down on the extremely comfortable sofa.

Malik stared at the scissors, then at Jina. "That's not fair," he told her, walking over to the sofa to stand over her. "Those tabs weren't on the other diapers."

She laughed, shaking her head. "That's the story you're going with?" she asked, lifting Lika up for a kiss.

Malik glared down at her, irritated that she wasn't intimidated. "Absolutely. And there's no evidence to prove otherwise," he stated with finality, putting the scissors on a high shelf where Lika couldn't reach them accidentally.

"We need to talk," he told her firmly.

Jina felt like a completely different woman now that she'd slept for more than four hours, was showered and in beautiful clothes. And she admitted that a break from taking care of Lika had done her a world of good. She loved her daughter with all of her heart, but having some time alone, even just enough time to take a long, leisurely shower where she didn't have to race to take care of Lika, had made her feel human again.

She kissed Lika's tummy, causing the tiny girl to giggle. "What would you like to talk about?" she asked and kissed her tummy again. Jina was unaware of Malik watching the two of them, stunned by the sweet sound of his daughter giggling. He'd taken care of her all morning and afternoon but he hadn't heard her make that sound.

When there was only silence, she looked up at Malik. He was staring at her with a strange look to his eyes. "What's wrong?" she asked softly.

Malik jerked out of his trance, shaking his head. Sitting down across from the two of them so that he had a better view, he asked, "Tell me about her," he commanded.

Jina smiled slightly. This was the Malik she remembered. All alpha male and demanding. When they'd first met, he'd tried order her around, expecting her to be enthralled by his attention. But she'd just thought he was a handsome, arrogant jerk.

She looked at Lika who had one foot on each of Jina's knees, trying to stand. "You tried that tone of voice with me before. Remember how far that got you?"

Malik chuckled and leaned back in the chair. "I remember that you were eventually in my bed, screaming out your pleasure," he came right back.

Jina leaned back against the soft cushions, her mind instantly going back to that time and she rejected the allure. She couldn't go there! She had to make him safe! This man was...everything. And she couldn't have him. She had to be cautious and maybe, eventually, the threat would go away.

"Don't do that," Malik commanded, taking her hands and gently squeezing them to reassure her. "We're going to talk about this and figure out what is going on."

Jina shook her head. "No, Malik. We can't. I can't be here with you. I have to..."

"Aaron!" Malik called, interrupting whatever she'd been about to say.

The head of security instantly stepped into the room, walking towards his boss. He looked at Jina, his eyes intent. "Tell me whatever you can about the incident," the big, burly man said as he stood at the end of both sofas and looked ready to go into battle.

Jina opened and closed her mouth, not sure if she could trust this man. Her blue eyes slashed over to Malik and he nodded his head.

Shifting Lika on her lap, she compressed her lips. "Malik, why won't you trust me? I can..."

He raised his hand, stopping her from whatever she'd been about to say. "Because you want to run from this. I don't agree with that path. From what I can gather, someone has threatened my life. We have to confront people like this. If we let them threaten our lives, then we lose and I'm not willing to lose." He paused to let those words sink in. "Are you willing to lose me, Jina? Again?"

Her hands were rubbing Lika's back, trying to figure out the best thing to do, the best way to handle this. "Malik..."

"Tell me about the day, Jina. What was going on?"

She sighed. Malik had the tenacity of a pit bull. He wouldn't let this go. He would poke and poke until she told him everything. Taking a deep breath, she explained what had happened that day, about the pictures, the voice, everything.

When she was finished, Lika was sleeping on her chest and she looked at Malik, begging him to understand. "So, you see? I can't really..."

Malik shook his head. "Jina, you are my wife now. You will be returning with me to Sarkit and we will announce our marriage." He turned to Aaron. "Do you have enough? At least for now?"

Aaron nodded his head. "I have several ideas."

Jina's eyes widened with the other man's words. "You're not going to..."

Aaron quickly shook his head. "No. This will be done quietly. I will handle the details of the investigation myself." He turned to Jina and bowed. "I will also personally oversee the selection of your personal guards, Your Highness. And we will be extremely careful in the selection of someone to help with the care of Lika. She will not be harmed." With that, he bowed and walked out of the room.

Jina stared at the man, stunned that he'd bowed and at the way he'd addressed her a moment ago. "Why did he...?"

Malik watched the woman with his adorable daughter, smiling as Lika slept despite the tension in the room. "Because you are my wife now, Jina. He addressed you with the formality that your title requires."

Jina shook her head. "That's crazy."

He raised a dark eyebrow. "No, Jina. That is protocol. Get used to it."

He stood up. "Aaron is making arrangements for us to return to Sarkit. I was supposed to be back already. You and Lika will be with me this time."

Jina's heart was pounding hard. "No! Please, you can't..."

He wasn't going to listen to her protests. Not this time! And he would ensure her safety on this trip. No one would get close to her or his daughter! "It is done, Jina. I will not abandon my family."

A knock sounded on the door and Jina's eyes slashed in that direction. Aaron stepped in front of the doorway, spoke softly, then nodded as he was handed a large, black box. He locked the door again and walked over to

Malik. He opened the box and Jina gasped. The sparkles that were shining out of that box were nothing short of astounding!

"What is that for?" she asked, shifting Lika, who was now sound asleep for her afternoon nap, in front of her as if the tiny child could somehow protect her from the diamonds. Or more specifically, what the diamonds implied. "I can't..."

Malik ignored her protests and lifted a diamond ring up, examining the stone carefully. He nodded his head then set it aside. Looking again, he examined the other rings and found another that looked more like a wedding band but was covered in diamonds. Carrying both, he moved over to Jina and took her hand, ignoring her protests and holding her hand firmly when she tried to pull away.

With little effort, he slid both rings onto her slender fingers and Jina stared down at the sparkling weight. The rings were stunningly beautiful and she swallowed painfully. This wasn't happening! After all she'd done over the past year to protect him, to protect Lika, this couldn't be happening! She'd left her last engagement ring back at the palace when she'd left. This one was larger, more beautiful and she had to fight back the tears that threatened once again.

Malik saw the emotions in her beautiful blue eyes and touched her cheek. "Stop," he said softly, closing her fingers around the bands. "It will be okay. Trust me."

Chapter 9

Five days later...

Malik looked at the picture that had been stuffed into one of the contracts he was reviewing and felt as if someone had stabbed him. Whoever had sent the picture was going to die! It showed a knife laying right next to his precious Lika! Impossible! How could someone have gotten close enough to his daughter?

"Aaron!" he roared, laying the picture down on his desk because he couldn't handle touching it any longer.

The head of security came rushing into the office, gun drawn and looking for the threat. When he didn't see anything, he lowered his weapon just as the other guards came rushing through the door.

With only one look from Malik, the head of security understood that something else had happened. Something that wasn't good.

Malik glared at the other guards. "Get them out," he told Aaron.

The men immediately filed out, closing the door behind them. Aaron walked over to Malik's desk, still not sure what was going on.

"Your Highness?" he prompted.

Malik leaned over, bracing his hands on the desk. He took in several breaths, then turned the picture around.

He heard Aaron's sharp intake of breath as well.

Malik was so angry, he was shaking with his fury. "I'm calling in help."

Aaron's teeth ground together. "I'll find out how this happened."

Malik's whole body was tense, ready to fight, ready to do battle but he didn't have an enemy to attack and it made him furious.

He lifted his phone and dialed a number. "I need help." That was all he needed to say and Aaron understood.

"I'll get her ready."

Malik rubbed his face. "Don't let her know. And because we must keep her in ignorance, she will be furious. She'll be hurt beyond belief." He bowed his head. "I'll send her to…" he thought frantically, not sure where to hide his family.

Thousands of miles away, four other men were canceling meetings and jumping into limousines while their private jets were fueled, preparing for the flight. One man was calling a woman who immediately scrambled to follow his request for help, calling in favors, stuffing boxes with the items she would need and conferring with several experts. When it was all packed, ready to go, she rushed out the door, calling her current clients to let them know that their projects would be delayed due to a family emergency.

Chapter 10

Jina stared at the head of security, not sure what he was telling her. "I'm sorry, but could you repeat that?"

"You have to go," Aaron said, "and it has to be fast." His eyes tried to convey a silent message but he obviously wasn't getting through.

Jina continued to stare at the man, still not sure what he was saying to her. "Explain to me what's going on."

Aaron shook his head. "Just get your stuff, grab the baby, and we're getting out of here."

Jina's heartbeat tripled in time. Something was wrong, and no one was telling her what was going on. "Tell me that Malik is okay."

Aaron hesitated for just a moment but it was enough that Jina caught it. It was the very first time that this man had ever hesitated in her presence, and that terrified her. The fact that he had hesitated, even for a moment, showed how flustered Aaron was. This man was never flustered. The fact that he was now, well, that really terrified her.

Calm, she told herself. She had to remain calm and figure this out, once and for all. "Okay, so here's what we're going to do. You're going to tell me what's going on. And you will tell me now. I'm not leaving, because something is going on and my husband is in jeopardy."

Aaron realized his mistake and was determined to do whatever it took to keep this woman safe. He shook his head after her words, ready to get her to safety any way he could. "No, Your Highness, I'm only here to help you leave the palace. His Highness says that he doesn't want you anymore. I'm only here to do his dirty work."

Jina ignored that statement, knowing that it was a complete fabrication. She continued to stare at the head of security, knowing that Malik didn't trust anyone more than he trusted this man. Malik was no coward. If he wanted her gone, he would be right here, sending her on her way. Malik could be one of the most heartless men she'd ever met in her life. Of course, with her, he was one of the most tender, gentle and loving men that she'd ever known. He would never do this to her. He might lie and tell her that something was…

Her blue eyes flashed up to Aaron's, quickly understanding what was happening. "He's in trouble isn't he?" Jina reached behind her and grabbed the chair, holding on for support because her knees were no longer able to hold her up. "The voice," she said, her own voice becoming horse as she figured out what was going on. "Someone got to him, didn't they?"

Aaron shook his head. "Your Highness, please," his voice went lower as the urgency came through in his tone, "just get your stuff and let's get out of here."

Jina glanced over at her daughter who was sleeping in the small crib. "Take care of my daughter!"

Jina didn't wait for Aaron to agree or disagree. She sprinted out of the room, knowing that something was wrong.

As she raced down the hallway, her mind started racing as well. She tried to imagine what was going on, why Malik was pushing her away. Obviously, he was trying to hide her away from some sort of danger. Jina wasn't going to allow that. Malik and her daughter were her life now. She'd been stupid to run the first time. She should have been honest with Malik, taken the initial pictures to him and demand that he fix the problem, keep them safe. Keep himself safe!

She wasn't going to run this time. Jina was going to figure this out. No more hiding, no more running, no more allowing someone else to destroy her family. This was going to end!

Tonight was supposed to be a special night between the two of them. She'd already spoken to the palace chef and they were busy preparing a meal for just the two of them. Aaron had agreed to watch Lika and she was going to make love to her husband. It had been way too long since she'd held him in her arms.

She hadn't wanted to come back here until the culprit had been caught, but Malik had insisted. So now he was going to deal with it and he wasn't going to do it alone! She was with him the whole time now.

Out of breath and trembling, she stopped running before she came to the administrative offices, not wanting to alert anyone in Malik's office if they were the ones doing this horrible thing to her family.

Taking a deep breath and trying to calm herself down, she put a hand to her chest and concentrated. This was too important to mess up. She had to look normal. She had to act as if there was nothing wrong, like her entire world was not about to be destroyed by some horrible individual with an agenda that didn't mesh with her husband's.

She forced her lips into a smile as she greeted the other guards standing sentry outside of her husband's office. "Is he in there?" She asked softly.

Both men hesitated, but they moved away. Thankfully, she hadn't been back long enough for protocol to be established for her visits so they didn't stand in her way when she wanted to see her husband.

Jina stepped through the heavy door and closed it behind her, gripping the doorknob tightly. Slowly, ever so slowly, Malik lifted his head. Before his eyes lit upon the intruder, he was about to bark out in order. In his current state of mind, whoever had dared to enter his office might have been imprisoned. But there she was, his beautiful wife, standing there trembling. For a moment, he just looked at her, staring at her beautiful features one by one, memorizing all of her.

And then he remembered the photograph. Hiding all of his love for this woman, he forced his lips to sneer. "So, you've come for one last quickie?" He said snidely, bracing himself when he noticed her body cringe.

Jina stared at the man she loved more than life itself. "What did you just say?"

Completely sober now, Malik stood up and walked around the edge of his desk, allowing his eyes to move up and down her body, pretending as if he wasn't interested. He took in a deep breath and said, "I'm sorry Jina, but I'm just not in the mood." And he turned around. Closing his eyes, he refused to allow himself to turn and take her into his arms. He had to get her out of here. Fast. His friends were on their way and he'd quickly be able to sort this out. Until then…

Jina couldn't believe what he had just said, neither of his statements. None of this was making any sense. "Yes, I'm here for a quickie." She watched carefully, trying to discern what he was saying to her.

Malik turned around and looked at her, shaking his head. "Sorry honey, I'm not interested anymore."

Jina tried to ignore the crushing feeling that surrounded her heart. This wasn't right! Malik was not like this! "You have never said anything like that to me before. In fact, I would wager that you've never said anything like that to any woman."

Malik chuckled. "Well, there's a first time for everything." He pulled a stack of papers closer to him and sat down in his large leather chair, stacking his feet up on his desk "Was there anything else?" And he shifted some papers.

Jina's hands were fisted at her sides as she listened to the horrible words. "Stop it! Just shut up! I know something is wrong and I'm going to figure it out!"

Jina spun around and swung open the door, rushing through and ignoring the guards that watched her abrupt departure.

This wasn't happening! Not again!

She ran down the hallway back to their private suite of rooms. No, Malik was not doing this to her. To them.

Aaron stood holding Lika. "Are you ready?" he asked. He was standing amidst a pile of luggage, obviously some of hers and also some of her daughter's. Jina didn't stop to wonder how she'd accumulated so much luggage in the short time since Malik had re-discovered her. There were more important things to deal with.

Jina ignored the man and started pacing back and forth, biting the tip of her thumb as her mind sorted through the information she had. Something was going on. This couldn't be happening.

She stopped moving, because something just occurred to her. Malik had never actually said that he loved her. He'd said that he wanted her. He'd told her in so many ways that they were sexually compatible. But had he ever actually said the words?

Jina realized that she'd only been assuming that he loved her. Malik had never said the words. This infuriated her, and it hurt. More than she wanted to admit.

Okay, so he didn't love her. But did he really have to push her away like this?

"We have to leave." Aaron didn't wait for an answer anymore. He was carrying the infant in his arms. Five servants appeared almost immediately and lifted the suitcases. All of them immediately followed Aaron out of the room, leaving Jina just standing there, her heart aching and her body trembling as the realization that Malik was pushing her out of his life.

No, no, no, no, no, no!

Jina shook her head, this was not happening!

The plane was taxing down the runway and a moment later, they were flying through the air, speeding away from the man that she loved. Looking down at Lika, Jina wasn't sure about anything. She suddenly realized that she didn't even know where the plane was going, why it was leaving, why Malik had pushed her away. Nothing made sense.

She stood up and started pacing the length of the plane. Thankfully, this was a very large, well-appointed private jet and she had plenty of space to walk back and forth. Biting the end of her thumb, she walked back and forth, her mind going over every detail. She thought about the events of the night, the morning, everything that it happened since she'd woken up this morning.

Shaking her head, she just didn't understand any of this.

The only thing that made sense…

Chapter 11

Malik closed his eyes as he leaned against his heavy desk after Jina's departure. "She understood!" he muttered softly. The damn woman was going to get herself killed because of that understanding. He leaned his open arms against his desk palms flat on the wood as he closed his eyes, praying that Jina wouldn't do anything that would get herself killed. Please, just let her be safe, he prayed.

Aaron walked into Malik's office and hesitated for a moment. "She's gone," he said carefully.

Malik nodded his head and pushed himself up off the desk. "Thanks. Now find the bastard who is doing this!"

Aaron nodded his head, his lips compressing as he turned around, obviously heading towards the security offices.

Three hours later, several large men walked into the private suite of rooms where Malik was slowly getting himself drunk. Stefan, Damon, Grayson and Harrison all stared at their friend with growing concern as Malik slammed back another shot of whiskey.

"What's going on? Harrison demanded immediately.

Malik laughed, feeling better now that his friends were here. "Where is Scarlett?"

The door open and closed behind the four men and they all heard an, "I'm here," the blond woman said as she stood in front of the four men. "And you're drunk. Interesting turn of events."

All five of them knew that something was seriously wrong if Malik was getting drunk. "Where is Jina?" Scarlett demanded.

Malik chuckled "Just like you to get right down to the heart of the issue, isn't it?"

"Are you going to tell us or are we going to have to beat it out of you? Damon asked. Not that any of them would lay a hand on Malik, not when he was in this state. They preferred to administer their beatings when all of them were fully functional and could fight back. At least, that's the way they used to do it. The only time they beat each other up now was when they were trying to have fun these days. Their boarding school fights were long past, thanks to Uncle Charles.

"Are we alone?" Malik asked.

The five other occupants of the room turned and looked at each other, startled that the man would even ask such a question. But they looked around, just to make sure. The only other person who had been allowed in this room was Aaron, the head of Malik's security team. But he had left as soon as he noticed that Malik was getting drunk. Aaron knew about the six of them, had observed their get-togethers over the past several years. The head of security knew that these six people were not a threat to each other.

Scarlett crossed her arms over her chest and glared at the man who took another slug of whiskey. "Tell us what is going on, Malik," she said. Scarlett moved closer, her crystal blue eyes looking into the darker ones of Malik's. She laid a hand on his arm, trying to stop him from slamming down another shot of whiskey. "Tell us what we can do."

Malik shook his head. "Someone is trying to kill me if I remain married."

That news startled everyone but the man draining his glass. They all knew that a year ago, he'd been a mess when his fiancée had disappeared suddenly. All of them had been making plans to attend his wedding and, suddenly, it was not happening.

Now they show up and he announces…

"Does that statement mean that you're married to Jina now?" Scarlett asked, watching him carefully.

Malik stood up and headed over to the bottle of whiskey in the corner. "A few days ago." He chuckled as he filled up his glass. "No wedding night though!"

He turned around but wasn't aware of Harrison who grabbed the drink out of Malik's hands. "Thanks old chap. Don't mind if I do," and he walked away with the glass in his hand.

Damon smiled. "I'll have more glasses delivered. Sounds like there's a lot to catch up on." He walked over to the door and gave instructions to the bodyguard.

"So where is the beautiful woman?" Stefan asked, taking a seat across from Malik. The others all settled in for a long chat, knowing that it was going to be difficult to get the truth out of Malik in this state.

At that moment, Aaron walked back into the room. "Have you all been briefed?"

Scarlett sat down next to Grayson but with several inches between their bodies. "Where are your wives?" she asked of Harrison, Stefan and Damon.

Damon answered for all of them. "They are meeting your plane in Athens. They will take care of Jina for you until we get this sorted out."

"Need Jina and Lika," Malik growled furiously, wanting to pound his fist into the wall because his newly discovered family was not here, under his roof and under his protection.

There was silence in the room as the others tried to figure out who Lika is. Scarlett leaned forward, her eyes narrowing. "Malik…" she started to say.

Fortunately, Aaron was much more aware of what had just been implied and he shook his head. "Lika is his six month old daughter," he explained.

Even more stunned silence!

Scarlett was the first to recover and she jumped up and ran over to give Malik a hug. "That's awesome news! When do we get to meet this little lady?" she asked.

The others all laughed as well, offering their heartfelt congratulations.

Malik's face was grim. "She's gone. Jina is gone. I had to send them away."

Aaron once again stepped forward and explained the situation. He tossed the pictures onto the table and all heads but Malik's leaned forward, Scarlett gasping in horror while the others turned furious.

Grayson and Damon stepped away from the group. The two men mumbled a few words to each other, then nodded. Scarlett lifted her phone to her ear and gave instructions. Several moments later a new man stepped into the room, a large suitcase in his hand.

Malik saw Aaron looking into the room, concern in his eyes. Malik shook his head. "It's okay Aaron. These men are safe. Go get me the information that I need."

Once again, Aaron nodded his head and stepped away from the door, giving orders to the guards outside to let no one else into the room unless His Highness approved it.

Grayson nodded to the man with a suitcase. "Do your stuff," Grayson said to the man.

The man nodded his head and opened the suitcase, immediately getting to work. Grayson walked over to the others, nodding his head and silently giving a message. "So our friend wants to get drunk. Why don't we help him?" But the silent message in Grayson's eyes contradicted that statement.

Instantly all the others understood what was going on. Damon, Stefan and Harrison lifted their glasses towards Malik. "To your freedom," they all said.

A moment later, the stranger in their midst walked over to Grayson and handed him something. Grayson looked down at the small disc in his hand, understanding exactly what it was. He stretched out his hand to show the others what he was holding. The others nodded their heads and continued talking, teasing Malik about his newfound freedom. The others watched Malik carefully, thinking that he might have had too much to drink in order to carry on the subterfuge. But their friend rallied, shaking his head in stunned reaction to the evidence in front of him. "I can't..."

Damon interrupted, "What about that woman that we saw last month?" he said, his eyes relaying a message as they slid over to the door that had just been closed. "She might be a good option," he said.

Malik's eyes narrowed. He glanced to the doorway, then back to Grayson's hand that was still open and holding the microphone. "I doubt it. My head of security is a bit wary of women coming into the palace right now. And I think that I have to agree with him. Not that there isn't something that we can do about my predicament," he said. Malik's head shook again, his eyes still not believing the evidence in front of him.

The man walked over and dropped another one in Grayson's hand and all of them stared in stunned silence once again.

After a few more moments, they all came back to their senses and realized that they should be talking. Grayson carefully placed the two small listening devices on the table in front of them while each of them sat down and started talking. The conversation seemed as if it was about nothing, but these men and Scarlett knew each other well enough that they could read between the lines and understand what was being said without the specific words. It was almost as if the six of them had their own code.

As they seemingly chatted about inane subjects, the man placed two more of the bugs on the table and kept on working. After about a half hour, the man turned around and nodded, indicating that he was finished with this room.

Grayson nodded back to the man. "Thanks for your work. I don't think that Malik will be needing your services at this point, but keep in touch. Maybe Malik can refer you to Aaron, the head of his security team."

The man silently nodded his head and walked out of the room. The remaining occupants of the salon stared at each other. They all knew what had to be done. The only questions remaining were how they were going to do it.

Malik stood up and rubbed his hand over his face, shaking his head with both fury and confusion.

"I think I need to go for a swim." A moment later, Malik walked out of the salon and disappeared into his private suite. The others all nodded their heads in agreement. At that point, they too stood up and walked out. Over the years, during their visits with to the palace, they had each been assigned a private suite, the same one each time they visited. So when they separated down the long hallway, their clothes had already been unpacked and stood waiting in the appropriate rooms. They each donned a bathing suit, grabbed a towel and walked out of their suite, ready to meet up and go for a swim.

Everyone met poolside at the back of the elaborate palace swimming area. The pool at this palace would be the envy of any five-star resort in the world. There was a lazy river and palm trees as well as an area for swimming laps. To the sides there were several different Jacuzzi areas and even a beach section so that little kids could wade into the water in a safer environment.

The objective now was not exercise. After finding all of the listening devices in the private salon, a place where no other communication devices should be found. The six of them dove into the water and met in the middle of the pool.

"Go change your clothes!" Grayson grumbled when he noticed Scarlett's black, two-piece bathing suit. The material covered all of the essential places and, in other people's minds the bathing suit might be conservative. But in Grayson's eyes, her bathing suit revealed way too much to his starving eyes.

Scarlett glared up at the obnoxious man. "We have more important things to discuss than your ridiculous, puritanical ideas on what a woman should wear while swimming."

Damon, Stefan and Harrison chuckled, but they settled down as soon as they caught Malik's serious expression.

"What were you able to find out?" Malik demanded.

Grayson pulled his eyes away from Scarlett, rubbing his face with frustration and trying not to let his body react. He was in a damn pool! His reaction would be pretty obvious!

"My team looked into Aaron first, but found that he was clean. We then looked at a couple of the guards who were assigned to Jina a year ago. One of the men has some sketchy details in his background."

Damon stepped in at that point. "After Aaron was cleared, my men talked to him about this other guy. His name is Musef and he was brought onto the security staff two years ago. Nothing ever happened before last year. But that's when he was able to afford a new car. Nothing outrageous, so it didn't raise any flags."

Harrison moved the water around his body as he said, "Aaron and my security team are watching Musef and a couple of others that he seems to be working closely with, trying to find out who they are meeting. I don't think that Musef is in charge. He's just the one that is trying to manipulate you."

Stefan agreed. "My team is providing backup for the surveillance. While we're inside the palace, my team will be working with Harrison's to try and determine who's at the heart of all this. In the meantime," he turned and looked at Scarlett, "you're going to go through the rest of the palace with our guy and find any other devices, correct?" He turned to the others. "Malik has asked Scarlett to redecorate the palace. It's going to be a thorough change of décor."

Scarlett smiled, ignoring Grayson's growl, and nodded her head. "Oh, you're going to love what I'm going to do with your suite, Malik. And now that I have a little girl to decorate for, well, you just wait and see! It's going to be amazing!"

Malik chuckled, having complete trust in her style. And her idea to pass off the "sweeper", the man who can find the other listening devices, as one of her assistants, was brilliant. "I'm glad you use your powers for good and not evil," he teased. Turning to Damon he asked, "Any idea on the origin of the pictures?"

Damon nodded his head. "I have my technical team working on that. One of them is definitely photoshopped. I have a guy looking at the others. He's checking the pixels, trying to determine how the images were created."

Malik's shoulders relaxed slightly. He knew that this group would take care of things. "Okay, so we all know what we're doing." Malik looked around at all the men, as well as Scarlett, an enormous sense of gratitude overwhelming him. These five people had dropped everything that they were doing simply because he called them and said that he needed help. He hadn't even taken the time to tell them what kind of help he needed. They just showed up.

Soon, very soon, he was going to get his wife and baby back. And it was all thanks to these people.

Chapter 12

Jina lifted Lika out of her carrier. The plane had landed and her tiny little daughter was eager to be doing something other than playing with her toes and her fingers. Jina still had no idea where she was and neither the flight attendant nor the pilot would tell her.

She peered out of the plane as soon as it taxied to one of the gates. Unfortunately, the gray skies and busy airport still didn't give her any clue as to which city she had been flown into.

"Jina!" A female voice said off to the side.

Jina turned her head and found two beautiful brunettes and one with beautiful, sandy-blond hair coming towards her. One had thick dark hair that streamed down her slender back and over her shoulders. The other one had softly curling brown hair while the blond laughed at something the others said. All of them with their designer suits and beautiful shoes made Jina feel more than a little frumpy. She'd just spent the last twelve hours on a plane and had no idea where she was, needed a shower and a good night sleep. Oh, and an explanation for what was going on would be wonderful! What she didn't need were problems in the form of beautiful women who made her feel inadequate.

And she was still furious with Malik for doing this to her and Lika!

"I'm sorry, but do I know you?" she asked, trying hard to keep the anger and impatience out of her tone but suspected that she'd failed.

The women only smiled more brightly. "You've got it bad, eh?" The black haired woman turned to the brown haired lady. "It is Malik, though."

The blond woman rolled her eyes. "Don't go there!"

They both laughed and Jina tried to tamp down her fury. "I'm sorry but…"

The brown haired woman extended her hand. "I'm Livia. I married into the group. This is Sierra," she explained, motioning to the blond woman, "and Sasha," the raven-haired woman extended her hand to Jina. "We're all married to one of the guys in the group."

Jina blinked while she accepted each woman's handshake with her free hand. "The group?"

Livia and the black haired woman grimaced while the blond laughed again, a beautiful sound that filled the air with music. "The group. You'll understand soon enough. But right now, we need to get you to a safe place. Malik's orders."

"How do you know Malik?" Jina demanded, thinking that if her husband had sent her into the care of his former lovers, he was in big trouble!

The black haired beauty laughed. "Not what you are thinking, I promise!" Jina realized that this woman was pregnant, but not very far along. Just enough to show a bit. "Would you mind if we explained everything in the car? We're a bit exposed out here and Malik wanted you safe."

Jina shrugged but followed the three women to the limousine that was waiting several feet away.

When they were ensconced in the privacy of the vehicle, the women turned to ooh and ahh about Lika. "And what is this little girl's name?"

Jina strapped her daughter carefully into the car seat, soothing her since she was tired of being strapped in. "This is Lika. Malik's daughter." As she strapped her baby girl into the car seat, the diamonds on her wedding rings flashed and she had to fight back the tears that threatened. Would she ever see him again? Would he push her out of his life just to keep the two of them safe as she'd done a year ago? She wasn't sure she could survive without seeing him.

The vehicle started moving and Jina turned to face the three women. "Could you please help me understand what is going on?" she begged.

Livia touched Lika's foot, wiggling the tiny appendage to distract the tiny human before she released a bellow of protest.

Sasha took over the explanations. "Here's the deal. We're supposed to keep you safe with us until the men get back."

"What men?" Jina demanded. "And safe from whom?"

Sasha shrugged. "The men are our husbands, the five who make up the group plus Scarlett, who is the only woman who has ever been allowed to get close to the guys until we each came along. Scarlett is wonderful. You'll love her as soon as you meet her and we're going to need your help trying to get her and Grayson, another member of the group, together. As for who we are supposed to keep you safe from, well, that's the million-dollar question. We don't know. I don't think Malik knows yet. But the entire group dropped everything…"

Jina was becoming impatient. "What group?" Jina demanded, frustration coming out in her voice. "I don't know anything about a group."

Sierra smiled, understanding Jina's impatience because each of the ladies had felt that way before. "You'll get used to all of this," she explained. "There are five men and Scarlett who is much younger than the guys. They all met in boarding school about twenty years ago and they've been fast friends ever since."

Sasha grinned. "They're horrible. Every one of them. But I guarantee that you're going to love them just as much as we do."

This was all very confusing. "And you're married to one of the members?" Jina asked.

Livia nodded, blushing for some reason.

"So are you," Sasha explained.

This was news! "What do you mean?"

"Malik is a member of what Livia and I started calling 'the group'. They stick together, they fight together, they do business together." Sasha laughed and waved her hand in the air. "The amount of wealth those men control is just disgusting," she said and shook her head. "Suffice it to say, that no one messes with one of them without messing with all of them. So when Malik called earlier today…"

Jina's body tensed with that news. "He called this morning?" She looked out the window, "What day is it anyway? Where are we?"

Sasha and Livia looked at each other. "Malik didn't tell you where he was sending you?"

Jina shook her head. "It was a bit…chaotic this morning." She looked down at Lika who was watching the newest faces carefully while one chubby fist clung to her mother's finger. "One moment, we were about to have breakfast, the next, Malik was telling me that I had to get out of the palace, that he didn't want me any longer."

Another look passed between Livia. Sierra and Sasha. They quickly turned back to Jina. "Don't believe it for a second. Malik was furious that there was a danger to you and he worked quickly to make sure you were safe."

Jina took a deep breath and fought hard to control her tears. "I didn't believe it. I was hurt initially, but once I figured out what was going on, I was angry with him. But I did this to him a year ago so I understand what he's dealing with."

Sasha leaned forward, placing her hand over Jina's gently. "I didn't know Malik a year ago, but there's one thing I know about him now. When he gives his heart to you, it is yours. He won't hurt you again. He's just trying to protect his family."

Jina had already figured that out but she was still hurt. "He should have done that with me and Lika there with him at the palace!" she said furiously. Her chin wobbled slightly until she could regain control. "I'm so angry with him!"

Livia and Sasha sighed while Sierra nodded her head sagely. "Oh, get used to this feeling. They will make you angrier than you could possibly believe," Sierra concurred, shaking her head.

"And happier," Livia commented with a smile.

"And everything in between," Jina grumbled.

All three women nodded their heads. "Just think what he's going to be like when Lika gets older!" Sasha commented.

Jina cringed. "Oh goodness, that isn't going to be good."

Again, the women shook their heads.

Jina sighed and leaned back in the luxurious vehicle. "So how do we deal with these guys?"

Sasha smiled and Livia chuckled. "Oh, we've learned various ways of getting around their irritating habits."

Jina looked at the three women, her respect and admiration growing exponentially. "How long have you been married?"

Livia touched the diamond ring on her finger, shaking her head. "Well, that's a long story." Sasha laughed at Livia's comment.

Sasha nodded her head with a laugh. "For both of us!"

Jina smiled for the first time in a long time. "I can't wait to hear about it." Sierra patted her arm. "The stories are a bit…crazy."

Sasha lifted a phone. "I think you probably need a good night's rest first of all. How about if we head back to my place and you can relax, let your little lady get out of that car seat and then we'll talk. I can't drink," she said, placing a hand over her tummy, "and I doubt you can."

Livia raised her hand. "I can!" she said.

The other women snorted and rolled their eyes. "Just you wait!" Sierra replied.

"Oh, I can't!" Obviously, Livia was eager to join the ranks of the pregnant.

The limousine pulled up outside of a gorgeous, villa style house and Sasha led the way inside. The interior was cooler than one would think and filled with stunning antiques that looked comfortable and inviting.

Sasha led Jina and Lika up a curving staircase and into a large bedroom filled with windows and a bed that looked wonderfully comfortable. "If you're okay with Sierra, Livia and I, we could watch Lika while you shower and change?"

Jina considered that idea for only a moment before she released her daughter into the women's care. "I'll hurry," she told Sasha.

"Relax," Sasha countered. "We'll just be downstairs. We won't even leave the house. If she cries in any way, we'll come get you but until then, you just relax and take a long shower or even a nap."

Jina watched the lovely woman carry her daughter out of the room. Slipping off her shoes, she let her toes sink into the thick carpet, wondering why she trusted the women so completely. She'd just run from her husband's palace compound where there was obviously a threat to herself, her husband and her daughter and yet, she'd just allowed her daughter to be carried out of her sight by what was basically a perfect stranger.

But there was something about the three women that reassured Jina.

An hour later, she felt a hundred percent better. She was showered and changed into a comfortable pair of slacks and blouse. The time alone had revived her and she was now eager to find Lika and her new friends. She was tired, not sure if it was the jet lag or the fact that she should probably be asleep at whatever time of the day it was in Sarkit. But she'd been traveling so much over the past several days, her body was completely out of whack.

Stepping into a beautiful living room, she found her daughter entertaining the three women who had abandoned their shoes and suit jackets and were on the floor, playing with Lika.

"Hello again!" Livia said as soon as Jina stepped into the room. "You look better. Feel better?"

Jina laughed. "Much," she said and sat down, watching Lika smile and wave her pudgy arms. "Was she okay?"

All of them nodded emphatically. "She's a doll!"

Jina smiled. "Well, she is now. But wait until five o'clock rolls around. She becomes a little nutcase," she said and kissed her daughter's belly, causing the little girl to laugh and grab Jina's nose.

The ladies smiled while a very motherly housekeeper bustled into the room. "Look at you ladies!" she gasped. "What would the gossips say if they could see you like this?" she admonished. She looked down at Jina. "And you! You're royalty. Sitting on the floor!" She clucked even as she set the tray on the floor filled with snacks and drinks. "You wouldn't be sitting down there if your husbands were here," she said. But then she chuckled. "Of course, if those men were here, you'd probably all be upstairs and I'd have this baby all to myself," she said and lifted Lika into her arms. "I'm taking her now. She needs a bath and you ladies need to figure out how you're going to handle this mess."

And she was off, Lika in her arms and mumbling something that made Lika giggle.

"Chloe will take excellent care of Lika," Sasha assured Jina.

Jina smiled. "I'm sure she will. Thank you. But what did she mean?"

Sasha started to stand up but Livia and Sierra quickly jumped up and grabbed one of Sasha's hands, pulling the pregnant woman up.

"Thanks!" Sasha replied. "As for Chloe's meaning, we have to figure out how to get those men to hurry up with their mission and keep Jina, Malik and Lika safe."

"What do we have to do?"

The four ladies leaned forward, snacking on excellent local cheese and crispy crackers that had been baked by the village baker earlier this morning, making them extra delicious. "Well, first of all, we need to trust those men to know what they are doing. They're extremely intelligent and have been around a bit more than we have. But that doesn't mean we take things lying down."

Jina liked these two women even more. "Okay, I am inspired and in awe."

Livia grinned. "We have to be very creative to keep up with our men. Otherwise, they will try and walk all over us."

"And wrap us up in gauze so we don't get hurt," Sierra added.

"Or send us away when things get difficult," Jina snapped, still furious with Malik for doing this to her. And she was furious with herself for allowing him to do this. She should have fought him, argued with him and she really should have stood her ground. But when it came to Malik, she wasn't sure how to think properly around him. The man was too smart for his own good and knew how to get to her.

With the help of these three ladies, she was determined to turn the tables. She was his wife! He could not protect her from the world like this!

Chapter 13

Chloe coddled Lika while the ladies sat around the dining room table, clicking away at brand new, powerful computers and with a growing array of papers taped all over the walls showing the results of their investigation.

"I found something else," Livia said, her eyes scanning some information. "Here, I'll print it out."

The four of them read through the details, nodding their heads. "That makes sense," Sasha agreed. The caption on the news article explained how leaders in Sistrain, the country more inland from Sarkit and having no ocean or water exits, was causing trouble with other countries. Nothing overt towards Sarkit that the ladies could uncover. Yet. But Sarkit was much more powerful than the other countries. And with Malik at the helm of Sarkit, there were implications from the Sistrainian government about how they weren't willing to rock that boat. Yet.

Jina tapped a pencil against her nose. The four of them had been working almost non-stop for the past ten hours. While the men were in Sarkit trying to discover the "who" of this mess, Sierra, Livia, Sasha and Jina were trying to figure out the "why".

Jina's eyes narrowed as Livia pinned the latest clue up on the board where they'd been building their case. "Okay, so make the connections."

The four of them continued to work well into the night, Jina taking time to feed Lika and cuddle with her, walking around the dining room where they were set up with Lika in her arms while they brainstormed. In fact, all four ladies did a bit of snuggling with the little girl, needing that connection and the innocence of her smiles or her sleeping face while they dug into the maliciousness of the world.

By the time the sun was coming up over the horizon, the ladies were exhausted but satisfied as they leaned against the table, surveying what they'd finally figured out. Around midnight, they'd started connecting strings to the various articles they'd pulled up and all of them were somehow tying back to members of the Sistrain government.

"Dougal?" Sasha called, wanting to show her bodyguard what they'd figured out.

The man stepped into the room, obviously having stationed himself right outside the dining room doors.

"What do you think?" she asked, pointing to the board with all of the connections.

Dougal looked through the information, his eyes widening as he took in all of their research. "This can't be right," he mumbled. But even as his eyes continued to scan the words, he was dialing a number on his cell phone.

"I'm putting you on speaker," he said when his boss came onto the line.

The women explained the progression of their investigation and the men at the other end of the line interrupted often to clarify or ask additional questions.

After thirty minutes, there was silence before Damon's head of security said, "Okay, I'm bringing this to Mr. Galanos. Standby. I'll call you back if we need more."

Chloe walked in at that moment with steaming cups of coffee. "I know you ladies have been awake all night. But it is time to take a break," she ordered. "Dougal, you too. Sit," she commanded.

Everyone sat down. She then poured coffee or herbal tea into each of the cups and passed them around. "I have breakfast in the oven but you're all going to have some fruit first. You need a healthy start to the day," she announced.

Lika, who had been sleeping at the other end of the dining room, Jina not wanting her daughter out of her sight as the four of them sifted through information on the dregs of humanity, started to make her presence known. "I'll take care of the wee one," Chloe announced and walked over to the bassinet, lifting the little girl into her arms and cooing to soothe the infant. "Oh yes, you need a new diaper and a full belly, don't ya?" she announced.

The baby girl clasped the housekeeper's red cheeks with her hands, in full agreement with all of the suggestions.

The phone rang just as Chloe was bringing out a cheesy egg casserole in one hand and Lika in the other.

"What have you found, love?" Damon asked, his voice serious but everyone could hear the concern in his voice.

The ladies once again explained their findings. They couldn't e-mail the links to his phone, not sure who might be intercepting data while he was at Malik's palace. When they were finished, they all heard his muttered curse. "I'll relay this to Malik." There was another pause before he said, "Ladies, this is incredible information. We've had a team following a suspect, but we couldn't get into this like you have been able to, not without alerting someone to our suspicions. You've turned a potentially weeks-long investigation into an overnight success." He laughed softly. "Sasha, when I see you again," he started, but he didn't finish his statement, leaving the rest of them to wonder what he meant.

But the pink staining his wife's lovely cheeks told each of them what his promise was and they smiled.

"Oh goodness," Chloe said. "They'll be in that bedroom all day long," she mumbled as she walked back into the kitchen, still retaining control of Lika.

"I don't think I'm going to be allowed to get a nanny," Sasha commented as she watched her housekeeper with her newest friend's daughter.

Jina laughed. "She's wonderful."

Sasha agreed. "Okay, how about if we take a break and shower, change into something more comfortable. I think a nap is in order. Anyone else?"

Jina wholeheartedly agreed. "But what about…"

Livia shook her head even as she stood up and stretched. "Don't even think about taking Lika out of Chloe's arms. That woman is in heaven and until you are able to get back to Sarkit, Chloe is that girl's grandmother."

Jina laughed again. "Okay. I'll nap and then come back and get her."

"There is a pool in the back if anyone wants to refresh that way," she offered as they each trudged out of the room.

Five hours later, Jina gasped as she sat up in bed. "Lika!"

A knock sounded on the door and Chloe slipped her head in the door. "Sorry to disturb your sleep, love, but this little one is getting a bit antsy. I've given her some food, but I think she wants her mother."

Jina sighed, pushing her hair out of her eyes. "Oh, Chloe, thank you for the break. I really needed some sleep and I'm so sorry for abandoning her to your care for so long."

"Oh nonsense. I loved having her with me. She's a dear!" The woman handed the little girl over, then turned and walked out. "I'm making some lunch and I want you and the little one downstairs as soon as you're finished."

Jina nursed Lika and enjoyed the quiet time with her daughter, but her mind was focused on Malik. She wondered if he was okay and prayed that she would get some information soon. It was miserable to not know where he was or if he was even alive. The men they'd researched the night before were bad men, willing to do anything to gain power in their country even if it meant bringing down Sarkit. Malik wouldn't let them do that, she knew, but to what lengths would he go to protect his country?

Very far, she knew.

Which only terrified her more.

Chapter 14

Malik stepped out of the limousine, almost tearing the door off of the hinges in his need to see his family.

The others stepped out more slowly, willing to give the man some time alone with his wife.

"Jina!" Malik shouted as soon as he stepped into the foyer of the peaceful villa.

Chloe stepped out of the kitchen, wiping her hands on her apron. "About time you arrived, young man!" she snapped. "And there's no use yelling. She won't hear you."

"Where did she go?" Malik demanded, already pulling his phone out, ready to get his plane refueled and back in the air. He wasn't wasting another moment. He wanted his family back beside him and he was going to move heaven and earth to make that happen.

"Oh pish," Chloe said and shook her head. "She's just out in the back with the other ladies in the pool. That adorable little girl of yours loves the water. One would think she was supposed to be a mermaid," the housekeeper chuckled. But she was now talking to herself because Malik was already rushing through the back doors, determined to find his family and hold both of his ladies in his arms.

As soon as he burst through the glass doors, he stopped cold. Four women, well, three women and one little girl, were splashing about in the pool, sunshine sparkling off of the crystal clear waters. Lika was the first to see him and her smile split her adorable, chubby face and her tiny hands splashed the water while her chubby legs wiggled underneath the floating circle that was holding her safely above the water. The rest of the ladies were a bit slower to react, but as soon as Jina saw him, she too burst into a smile.

But a moment later, that smile disappeared and her anger came back. "Don't you dare come any closer!" she told him.

Malik ignored her. He barely took the time to slip his shoes off before he dove into the water. In a swift movement, he lifted Lika and Jina into his arms. One of them was wiggling in order to get closer, the other was wiggling to get out of his arms but he held both of them securely even while he whipped his hair back and forth to get the water out of his eyes.

Kissing Lika gently on the cheek and nuzzling her nose, he then turned to smile down into Jina's angry eyes. "Hello, love."

"Don't you dare 'love' me you horrible bastard!"

Malik only chuckled and pulled her closer. "Ah, you love me. And you knew exactly what I was doing." He kissed her, harder this time. "As soon as you figured out what I was trying to do, you fixed it so that we could all be together again."

She was already trembling now, just from the one kiss. Jina tried to hold onto her anger, but he was grinning triumphantly and she couldn't resist this man. Never had been able to do it and now was no exception.

"I hate you."

"You love me. Otherwise, you wouldn't have found all of that information and gotten rid of the threat so quickly."

"It's over?"

"Yes. I found the culprit."

"Who was it?" she asked, staring up at him with wide, hopeful eyes.

"A guard named Musef was the man who threatened you a year ago," he explained.

That was startling news. "Musef?" she whispered, shivering at the realization that the man that who had been in charge of keeping her safe was the primary threat. "But why?"

"Money," he said simply. "He was bribed. Once you and the ladies here figured out the reason behind the threats, we were able to trace the money from Musef back to the Prime Minister of Sistrain. We wouldn't have figured it out if it weren't for the money trail and bugs."

Jina's eyes widened in surprise. "Listening devices?"

"Yes. They were all over the palace. Aaron tried to resign once they were discovered but I wouldn't let him go."

Jina leaned against his chest, unaware of Sierra, Sasha and Livia slipping out of the pool to be with their husbands. She only had eyes for one man.

"I'm glad that Aaron will stick around. He's a good man." She grimaced. "He just needs to learn to change a diaper," she laughed.

Malik threw back his head, laughing at the memory of how they'd taped the diaper on Lika. Turning to nuzzle his baby daughter's cheek, he said, "You didn't mind, did you?"

Lika's only response was to smack her baby hands on his cheeks.

Jina realized what he was wearing and pulled back. "Malik, you dove into the pool in your clothes!" she gasped.

He chuckled, delighted that his family was safe. "What's the problem?"

Jina thought about that for a moment. "I love you."

He bent lower to kiss her gently. "I love you too. And we're going home."

Her smile brightened. "Then I guess we don't have any problems, do we?" she sighed happily.

Excerpt from The Tycoon's Captured Heart, book 5 in The Boarding School Series

Slowly, the casket was lowered into the ground. Scarlett's handkerchief couldn't keep up with the tears, so she just allowed them to flow down her cheeks, ignoring the wetness as she tried to deal with the pain of losing the man who had become her second father.

She hated cancer! She hated the fact that it had taken yet another victim. Its merciless clutches were pulling yet another innocent, kind-hearted soul away from people who needed him.

Uncle Charles didn't deserve this! He shouldn't be dead! He should be right here next to her, next to all of them, threatening something horrible if… She had no idea what he might be saying and she was too sad, too grief-stricken to even think of something.

"Ashes to ashes, dust to dust," the minister said. She was motioned forward, handed a rose from one of the arrangements. Scarlett knew she should toss the flower onto the coffin, but she couldn't do it. She couldn't say this final goodbye.

Oh goodness! She'd thought she had said goodbye at the hospital just before he'd died but obviously, she hadn't finished.

"It's okay, love," Grayson said, his deep voice reverberating through her body with reassurance. His strong arm wrapped around her shoulders. That touch, that gentle reassurance, gave her the strength to release the flower. She watched it flutter into the hole, landing silently on the casket. Grayson's rose came next and they both moved on, allowing others to do the same. One by one, the mourners filed past, adding their flowers, their thoughts and prayers, silently saying their goodbyes.

When everyone had finally paid their respects, Scarlett stood there, surrounded by the numerous students who had been touched by this man's life as headmaster. So many people, so many lives changed because of this man's bountiful care. Uncle Charles had always been stern with discipline and demanding of excellence, but equally generous with his praise. He'd been headmaster of the boarding school for decades, constantly leading boys through a challenging and exciting time in their lives. But none were as affected as the five men who were lined up behind her.

Without Charles' intervention, she wasn't sure what might have happened to them. One was a British aristocrat, another a powerful sheik. The other three were extremely powerful in their own right. But one of them, the man with his arm around her shoulders, the man she…well, he might have ended up in prison if it hadn't been for Uncle Charles.

"You okay?" Grayson asked gently.

Scarlett looked up at Grayson, wishing she could simply lay her head against his broad, muscular chest. But that wasn't…they didn't…

She sighed. Grayson wasn't hers. Not in that way. No matter how much she might wish it.

Nodding, she accepted that this was the end of Uncle Charles' life. This was the real final goodbye. Uncle Charles, the man who had dropped everything to come get her after her parent's tragic car accident, was now gone from this life.

Reaching out, she felt for Grayson's hand. She needed his strength now and he never failed to provide exactly what she needed. No matter what she asked, Grayson was always there for her. She moved slightly closer, just wanting to feel the heat emanating from his large, muscular body. Grayson's warmth and strength surrounded her cold hand, just as it always had. She wanted to lean into him, but she stood tall, trying to be strong for the others.

But as she looked around, Scarlett remembered that the other four all had their wives! Damon, Stefan, Harrison…even Malik had a beautiful wife standing beside him.

She had Grayson. Sort of.

She loved this man more than anything. She'd loved him since she was twelve years old. Maybe even longer. There had always been something about him that had drawn her to him. The other guys, yes, they were wonderful. All of them were tall, strong, powerful and wealthy. Every one of them would drop whatever was happening in his life if she needed help.

But they were like her big brothers. They were big and tall and normally annoying, but also sweet and kind and shockingly generous. Oh, and she definitely needed to add that they were overly protective. To the point that they drove her nuts at times.

Grayson…he wasn't. He wasn't her brother. Not at all! He was big and tall and super powerful as well but he was…different. She didn't think of him in the same way as the others even though she'd grown up surrounded by all of them. And she could never think of the enormous brute as a brother. That special something about him called to her, made her whole body tingle with excitement whenever he stepped into a room.

Damn him! Why did he have to be so wonderful? So perfect! He was always there for her! When she was scared, she called him. When he had a success in business, she ran to him, eager to celebrate with him. When he bought a new house or penthouse apartment, she decorated it for him. She loved him. Every part of him, every emotion, every obnoxious, irritating, heavenly part of him.

But did he return those feelings? No! He thought of her as his baby sister, just like all the other guys. Well, she wasn't his baby sister! She was a grown woman with wants and needs!

From the moment Uncle Charles had revealed that he had cancer, all six of them, plus their wives now, had surrounded the man. Each of them, with their unimaginable wealth, had tried to save him, come up with a cure for the cancer that slowly taken his life away.

But none could save the dying man.

And now he was gone. His body was down in the cold earth and she wanted to scream at the injustice of it all. Grayson's hand slid under her hair, holding her head close as the grief shook her body. Well, at least she had this, she told herself.

Back at her house, Scarlett walked in and looked around, not sure what to do. She struggled to find something to say, some way to help each of these men. Damon, Harrison, Stefan and Malik all moved into the living room, holding their wives close. These men, including Grayson who stood aside, his hands in his pockets as he stared at the floor, had been like sons to Uncle Charles. The man had been the headmaster at their boarding school, had never given up on any of them even when they'd all deserved to be expelled for their constant, vicious fighting. It wasn't until Scarlett had shown up that the five of them had stopped fighting. Uncle Charles had said that Scarlett had saved their lives that day. But she'd been just five years old. She'd come from her parent's funeral and walked in to find the five of them fighting, all of them just a pile of swinging fists and flying feet. With her presence, they'd stopped the fighting. And with Scarlett's presence and the uniting force that it produced, the six of them had become best friends.

Oh, goodness, she remembered the day that they'd all graduated and gone off to college. It had been the second worst day of her life, her parent's funeral being the worst. But today ranked up higher than the day these five men had left her to go their own way.

Thankfully, the six of them, now ten with each of their wonderful wives, remained friends, coming together often to have a meal and catch up. Barely a month went by when several of them didn't get together. It used to be just a meal at a hotel or restaurant. Now that there were so many of them, the arrangements were a bit more complicated, but they all still got together as often as they could.

What was going to happen now?

She glanced over at Grayson, finding him staring right back at her. She wasn't sure what to think about that look.

And right now, she was too confused, too sad and hurt, to figure anything out.

"The other mourners will be here soon," she finally said, the first words spoken since the burial.

All of them nodded. "The caterers have prepared food." She took a deep breath and lifted her head. Looking into each man's eyes, she smiled. "Let's make this a celebration of his life and not..." her voice broke as she tried to speak and Grayson came over, putting his arm around her shoulders. Instantly, she felt better. "Let's not make this sad," she said even though her chin was still quivering. "Uncle Charles made a difference in so many peoples' lives. We should celebrate everything he was – not dwell on the fact that he isn't here any longer."

The men nodded their heads and Livia, Stefan's wife, stepped out of the room. She came back a moment later with a tray filled with champagne glasses and Scarlett smiled her thanks as each of them took a glass.

All of them stood in a circle, none exactly sure what to say. It was such a poignant loss and each of them experienced a deluge of emotions as they replayed memories of a man who had acted as a father to each of them, often more so than their actual blood relatives.

"To Uncle Charles," Grayson finally said and lifted his glass into the air. A mummer of agreement chimed around the group and ten glasses lifted up in a sad celebration. "To Uncle Charles," they all said, then sipped the cold, sparkling wine.

Two hours later, it was once again just the six of them. The men's wives had all gone to their hotel rooms and Scarlett was looking around at the five men, laughing at all of the stories, their memories.

This had been good, she thought, feeling better. Uncle Charles had died several days ago, and the time between then and now had been full of arrangements to make. Although the details had given her something else to concentrate on, before Uncle Charles died, she'd been by his side constantly, holding his hand. Now, talking about all of the wonderful times she and the others had shared with Uncle Charles, she felt better. The sadness was gone, replaced by a happiness that she'd been given so much time with the wonderful man.

For the first time in several weeks, she felt as if her heart was lifted. The sadness was gone. At least for now. She knew she'd have moments in the future, moments when she would miss him again, but for now, she could breathe easier. This was good. These men had helped, Grayson's touch had helped, and talking had brought about a form of healing.

She smiled as she sipped her whiskey, impressed when the others slammed back their drinks and held their glass out for more. For a while now, there had been only laughter between them, sharing fond memories of the man who had been so much more than their headmaster. Scarlett was curled up at the end of the sofa, her shoes long gone and the tears a distant memory. At least for now.

"You doing okay?" Grayson asked softly. He was sitting beside her but they weren't touching even though she'd like nothing better than to crawl onto his lap and lay her head on his shoulder. He wasn't drinking as much as the others, but he could still slam them back.

"I'm okay," she told him and was surprised that she really was. They'd all had months to get used to the reality of him dying, had slowly watched him lose the unbeatable battle with cancer and now, as they all sat around the living room, there was a sense of peace. A rightness in being together.

He took her hand, squeezing it slightly. It was a silent message that he was there for her.

A moment later, Malik stood up. "We need to go. Our wives will be wondering what's happened to us." He looked at Grayson. "Can you stay and take care of Scarlett?" he asked. The four other men stood, each of them looking at Grayson as well, as if they were trying to tell him something important.

"I'll be here," he said and stood up, keeping her hand in his. "For as long as she needs."

The four others reached out and kissed Scarlett's cheek, giving her their brotherly support. It was a wonderful feeling to know that these men were there for her. There was nothing they couldn't do, she thought. They were all so powerful, so amazingly intelligent and wealthy. Each of them was a force, but put the five of them together and it was like a powerful coalition. No one messed with these men!

And she loved them all!

When the door closed on the last one, she turned to find Grayson collecting the glasses. His tie had long ago been tossed to the side, his jacket was probably over a chair somewhere which meant that she had an unfettered view of the tailored material stretching across the muscular expanse of Grayson's shoulders. He was so well put together, she thought, still leaning against the door.

Grayson felt her eyes on him and looked across the living room to where she was standing, leaning against the front door. "What?" he asked, amusement in his eyes.

Scarlett sighed, wishing she had the courage to just tell him how much she wanted him to take her into his arms and make love to her. She shivered, thinking how he could touch her gently and her mind turned to mush.

He was probably dating someone again. She laughed at that, looking up at the ceiling, thinking of how ridiculous that thought was. Grayson didn't "date". He had mistresses. He had them tucked into apartments wherever he needed them.

"What's so amusing?" he asked as he carried the glasses to her kitchen. The room had clean lines and pretty colors, reflecting the owner's preferences. As an interior designer, Grayson knew that Scarlett tried very hard to make sure that the rooms reflected the owner's preferences. He should know. He'd bought many properties and allowed Scarlett the freedom to create. In every instance, she'd done an outstanding job. Most of her projects appeared in the decorating or home magazines and her business had grown exponentially in just the short amount of time that she'd been on her own.

Scarlett shook her head and glanced down at the countertop where the caterers had stacked up various serving platters and silverware. They'd provided most of the items for the reception, but she'd supplemented with a few of her own favorite pieces. Grayson didn't want to know what she was thinking though. He'd be uncomfortable if he ever knew all the fantasies starring his magnificent physique. "Nothing important. Thanks for your help cleaning up," she told him as she loaded up the dishwasher. "The caterers did most of the cleanup. Thanks for hiring them," she told him.

Scarlett turned around but she wasn't aware that Grayson had been so close. Suddenly, his muscular arms were around her waist, holding her steady and everything changed. He was here. His arms were around her. All the emotions and feelings she'd hidden from this man rose up, her mouth falling open as she realized at least a small part of her fantasy coming true. Now, if only he would…

In just her stocking feet, the top of her head didn't even come up to his chin. She stared at his neck, seeing his Adam's apple move slightly.

Looking up at him, seeing the same desire in his eyes that she was feeling, she wanted to shout at him to do something about it, to make a move.

But he pulled back, his hands slipping off of her waist.

Scarlett sighed with frustration. The moment was gone.

Someday, somehow she would build up enough courage to just walk up to him and kiss him, to show him how much she loved him.

Unfortunately, today wasn't that day.

"Go to bed," he told her, his deep voice huskier than normal. "I'll sleep in the guest room."

Scarlett gripped the edge of the countertop. "There's no need. But thank you."

Grayson saw the sadness in her eyes and reacted to it. There was no way he was letting her sleep in this house alone tonight. She was sad, exhausted, vulnerable and looking more beautiful than any woman he'd ever known in his life. "There's every need," he argued. "Go to bed, Scarlett."

Scarlett watched him for a long moment and thought she could detect a battle waging inside the man. Was she just imagining that? Or was she hoping that he was fighting the same demons, the same desire that she was battling?

In the end, she just walked out of the kitchen, bowing her head with both fatigue and frustration as she walked up the stairs.

Grayson watched the woman of his dreams, literally and figuratively, walk up the stairs, her shoulders sagging with the pain of her loss.

If he thought it would make a difference, he would take her into his arms and kiss her until she was shivering with excitement. But that was what *he* needed. Scarlett just needed a friend, someone to be there for her. She definitely didn't need a lust-filled night of sex. Sex that would take their minds off of the loss of the man they all loved very deeply.

When she turned the corner and he couldn't see her any longer, he bowed his head and tried to get a grip on this need. He'd wanted her for so long, he felt as if he was damned to eternal, unsatisfied sexual need. Every once in a while he would find a woman that he'd hoped would take his mind off of his feelings for the beautiful blond woman, but after a few weeks or, if he were lucky, a few months, he would accept that she wasn't Scarlett. So far, no woman had been able to obliterate his hunger for the slender blond with blue eyes that could look deep into a man's soul and make him want to be better.

He poured another slug of scotch and slung it back, wishing that it could help ease the need. It never did. Nothing helped. Nothing but a few weeks in a bed with that woman would help him.

And since that was out of the question, he was doomed.

"Hell," he muttered and went around the house, turning off lights and making sure the doors were locked. He glanced out through the windows and saw his bodyguards patrolling the perimeter. At least he could keep her safe, he thought. It wasn't much, but it was something.

When all the lights were turned off, he walked up the stairs, turning right and moving into the guest bedroom. It was decorated in masculine colors which soothed him. Not as much as being in her frilly bedroom might, he thought. He didn't give a damn what the bedroom looked like as long as Scarlett was curled up next to him. Or underneath him. Or on top of him.

"Hell," he said again and stepped into the bathroom, turning the water on in the shower so that it was as cold as possible. It only helped marginally. Stepping out of the shower, he dried himself off and slipped into bed.

Staring up at the ceiling, he wondered what Scarlett was doing. Was she crying? She'd buried her last relative today. It had been a long day, full of tearful remembrances as well as happy ones. It had ended well, he thought, overall. Would she still be upset?

And what the hell was going on with the other guys tonight? There had been some strange looks passing among them. He had no idea what was wrong, but they were all meeting for breakfast tomorrow. He'd demand answers as soon as he got them all alone.

Scarlett lay in bed, her eyes staring up at the ceiling and wondering what Grayson was thinking about. He was so close. What would he do if she slipped into his bed, curled up next to him? She'd decorated that bedroom with him in mind, making sure all the colors were dark and masculine, that the bed was long enough for his enormous height and that all of the toiletries were there for his convenience.

Would he find the toothbrush? And the shampoo he preferred? The only reason she knew which products he liked was because she'd stayed in his homes over the years. She'd snooped as she'd decorated his living spaces. And Scarlett savored every detail she discovered about the man. She'd felt like a stalker, but what was a woman to do? She was so in love with the man, so proud of all he'd accomplished. He was extraordinary and no other man could compare. His features were harsh to some, but she loved that granite hard jawline, that slight dimple in his cheek that not many people saw because it was only revealed when he smiled and Grayson didn't smile often. Oh, and that thick black hair, making his dark jaw even though he might have shaved just hours ago.

Goodness, everything about the man enticed her – from his broad shoulders to his large feet. She smiled into the darkness, wondering if the thing about feet and man-size was true. She could feel her face flaming even in the darkness and she rolled over, groaning at the image of a naked Grayson popping into her mind. Pulling the pillow over her head, she tried very hard to keep herself from thinking about him. About all those muscles and the way he could look at her and she knew…she just knew that he was thinking about her.

Oh to be inside that man's head, she thought.

Or maybe not. She didn't want to know if he still thought of her as a little girl. She was a woman now. And she had needs like any other woman!

She should just find another man to date. A blond man, she thought. Someone short and skinny. Someone who was easy to talk to.

The complete opposite of Grayson!

That wasn't completely true and she was simply creating problems with Grayson and her relationship with him to make herself feel better. There had been many times that she and Grayson had talked for hours! Just a few months ago at Stefan's wedding, it had ended up being just the two of them talking after everyone else had gone to bed. That had been nice, she thought. All the others had their spouses and had been eager to sneak up to their suites at the hotel, but she and Grayson had been…well, they'd sort of been stuck with each other. And it had been so nice, dancing in his arms, walking down the aisle on his arm. They'd just been bridesmaid and groomsman, but she'd pretended like it was their wedding, that she'd just promised her life to his and they would live happily ever after.

She sighed and the sound echoed throughout the room.

She wasn't ever going to get any sleep, she muttered.

Slapping the sheets back, she slipped out of bed. Listening carefully, she didn't hear anything. Noises from Grayson's room were silent now, indicating that he was asleep.

Slipping out of her room, she tiptoed down the hallway. She'd just made it to the top of the stairs when an arm swooped under her stomach, lifting her up and pressing her against the hallway wall.

"Scarlett?" Grayson snapped as soon as he realized it was her and not an intruder. "What the hell are you doing?"

Scarlett wasn't hurt but she was definitely stunned. The man wasn't wearing a shirt! And…well…she was wearing one of his!

"What are you wearing?" he demanded softly but with a definite husky quality to his voice when his eyes moved down her figure. His voice was even deeper as he said, "Hey, that's my shirt."

Darn him for the stupid monogrammed initials, she thought! "I…um…couldn't sleep. I was just going downstairs for some warm milk."

He looked down at her, not sure if he believed her or not. "Where did you get my shirt?" he asked.

He was trying very hard not to react, but her soft body felt so incredibly good against his. And he'd only paused to pull on his slacks before he came out of his bedroom to find out who was sneaking around the house. Never would he have imagined that it was Scarlett. In his shirt!

And she looked hot! Her long, slender legs were poking out the bottom and she hadn't buttoned it up high enough on top. He could see the curve of her breast, the shadow of her cleavage. Damn, she smelled good! Hell, she always smelled good.

"You couldn't sleep," he repeated, his mind trying to figure out what that really meant because the words weren't sinking in. Not with Scarlett in his arms, practically naked. And smelling better than anything he'd ever smelled before!

"I couldn't sleep," she whispered. She could feel her breasts swelling, her nipples puckering as she pressed against his hard, muscular chest. She could smell the musky, masculine scent of him and the toothpaste he'd used. His hair was still damp and...oh, that chest!

When her hands fluttered around then slowly settled onto his bare skin, she tested movement, feeling the warmth under the steel of his muscles. He was real, she thought. His skin was warm and amazing. Her fingers moved again, feeling the slight layer of dark hair and that felt even better.

She wasn't aware of her hips moving, shifting to accommodate him better. But she was desperately aware of his erection, of the way it pressed into her belly. From what she could feel, that thing about big feet...it was true!

"Grayson," she whispered his name, her body shifting once again, her fingers moving along his skin. He hadn't moved an inch except for his hands tightening on her waist.

She looked up at him, could barely see his eyes but she knew that they were a deep green, so special and so amazing. They saw everything.

"Would you..." she hesitated, unable to say the words that would bring his head down.

Grayson heard the strange sound in her voice and his body hardened even more. Could Scarlett possibly want him as much as he wanted her? Impossible. But then her hips shifted again. He felt her fingers move lower on his chest.

All the signs were there, but he still didn't move. He didn't release her, but he didn't react to the signs that, with any other woman, would have told him to lift her into his arms and make love to her. Not Scarlett. She didn't think of him that way.

And yet, her fingers moved again. He caught the look underneath those long, dark eyelashes even in the dim light from the moon outside the window.

With a growl, he bent his head, testing the signals. He wouldn't kiss her. Not like he wanted to. But just a chaste kiss. A kiss on her cheek. A brotherly kiss, he promised.

She moved her head, catching that kiss on her lips. He didn't move for a long moment but then her lips shifted under his. He felt that. For perhaps a fraction of a moment, he didn't move, didn't even breathe. But when her lips touched his, moving underneath his, he couldn't hold back. For too long, he'd fantasized about this woman, about the way she would feel in his arms. And as he lifted her up, he realized that she felt even better.

If you enjoyed this preview, look the book at your favorite retailer now! Also see ElizabethLennox.com for a free introduction to The Boarding School Series.

List of Elizabeth Lennox Books

The Texas Tycoon's Temptation

The Royal Cordova Trilogy
Escaping a Royal Wedding
The Man's Outrageous Demands
Mistress to the Prince

The Attracelli Family Series
Never Dare a Tycoon
Falling For the Boss
Risky Negotiations
Proposal to Love
Love's Not Terrifying
Romantic Acquisition

The Billionaire's Terms: Prison or Passion
The Sheik's Love Child
The Sheik's Unfinished Business
The Greek Tycoon's Lover
The Sheik's Sensuous Trap
The Greek's Baby Bargain
The Italian's Bedroom Deal
The Billionaire's Gamble
The Tycoon's Seduction Plan
The Sheik's Rebellious Mistress
The Sheik's Missing Bride
Blackmailed by the Billionaire
The Billionaire's Runaway Bride
The Billionaire's Elusive Lover
The Intimate, Intricate Rescue

The Sisterhood Trilogy
The Sheik's Virgin Lover
The Billionaire's Impulsive Lover
The Russian's Tender Lover
The Billionaire's Gentle Rescue

The Tycoon's Toddler Surprise
The Tycoon's Tender Triumph

The Friends Forever Series
The Sheik's Mysterious Mistress
The Duke's Willful Wife
The Tycoon's Marriage Exchange

The Sheik's Secret Twins
The Russian's Furious Fiancée
The Tycoon's Misunderstood Bride

Love By Accident Series
The Sheik's Pregnant Lover
The Sheik's Furious Bride
The Duke's Runaway Princess

The Russian's Pregnant Mistress

The Lovers Exchange Series
The Earl's Outrageous Lover
The Tycoon's Resistant Lover

The Sheik's Reluctant Lover
The Spanish Tycoon's Temptress

The Berutelli Escape
Resisting The Tycoon's Seduction
The Billionaire's Secretive Enchantress

The Big Apple Brotherhood
The Billionaire's Pregnant Lover
The Sheik's Rediscovered Lover

The Tycoon's Defiant Southern Belle

The Sheik's Dangerous Lover (Novella)

The Thorpe Brothers
His Captive Lover
His Unexpected Lover
His Secretive Lover
His Challenging Lover

The Sheik's Defiant Fiancée (Novella)
The Prince's Resistant Lover (Novella)
The Tycoon's Make-Believe Fiancée (Novella)

The Friendship Series
The Billionaire's Masquerade
The Russian's Dangerous Game
The Sheik's Beautiful Intruder

The Love and Danger Series – Romantic Mysteries
Intimate Desires
Intimate Caresses
Intimate Secrets
Intimate Whispers

The Alfieri Saga
The Italian's Passionate Return (Novella)
Her Gentle Capture
His Reluctant Lover
Her Unexpected Admirer
Her Tender Tyrant
Releasing the Billionaire's Passion (Novella)
His Expectant Lover

The Sheik's Intimate Proposition (Novella)

The Hart Sisters Trilogy
The Billionaire's Secret Marriage
The Italian's Twin Surprise (USA Today™ Best Seller!)
The Forbidden Russian Lover (USA Today™ Best Seller!)

The War, Love, and Harmony Series
Fighting with the Infuriating Prince (Novella)
Dancing with the Dangerous Prince (Novella)
The Sheik's Secret Bride
The Sheik's Angry Bride
The Sheik's Blackmailed Bride
The Sheik's Convenient Bride

The Boarding School Series – September 2015 to January 2016
The Boarding School Series Introduction
The Greek's Forgotten Wife
The Duke's Blackmailed Bride
The Russian's Runaway Bride
The Sheik's Baby Surprise
The Tycoon's Captured Heart

Made in the USA
Middletown, DE
29 December 2015